Joseph Cornish

The Life of Mr. Thomas Firmin

Joseph Cornish

The Life of Mr. Thomas Firmin

ISBN/EAN: 9783337333232

Printed in Europe, USA, Canada, Australia, Japan

THE
LIFE
OF
MR. THOMAS FIRMIN,
CITIZEN OF LONDON.

BY

JOSEPH CORNISH,

Pastor to the Church of Protestant Dissenters at Colyton, in the County of

DEVON.

The memory of the just is blessed. Prov. x. 7.

He was a man, take him for all in all,
We shall not look upon his like again. *Shakespeare.*

LONDON:

PRINTED FOR J. JOHNSON, NO. 72. ST. PAUL'S CHURCH-YARD.

1780.

TO

A GENTLEMAN,

WHO,

FROM EXTREME MODESTY,

WILL NOT PERMIT THE MENTION OF HIS

NAME;

WITH WHOSE ZEAL FOR THE CAUSE OF LIBERTY,

WITH WHOSE REGARD TO THE INTEREST OF RELIGION,

WITH WHOSE DELIGHT IN DOING GOOD,

THE AUTHOR OF THIS WORK IS WELL ACQUAINTED,

AND OF WHOSE BENEVOLENCE,

AND THAT OF SOME OF HIS NEAREST CONNECTIONS,

THE AUTHOR HATH ALSO HIMSELF LARGELY EXPERIENCED;

THIS ATTEMPT

TO DO SOME SMALL JUSTICE TO THE MEMORY

OF ONE OF THE BEST OF MEN

IS MOST RESPECTFULLY DEDICATED,

PREFACE.

NOTHING can be more worthy of a rational creature, than to endeavour, by every mean in his power, to promote the knowledge and practice of virtue. This is the professed aim of the moralist and the divine; and unless the philosopher and historian keep this end in view, their speculations and researches, though they may gratify the curiosity natural to the human mind, fail in that which is of much greater consequence;— the impressing upon it a sense of its true dignity, and exciting in the breast a desire of being and of doing good.

The study of history is very pleasing to the generality, and may be made the vehicle of conveying much of that useful knowledge which renders the heart

a 2 better.

better. Biography is a ſpecies of hiſtory which gives a writer ſome peculiar advantages, who would teach men to be good by examples. The hiſtorian muſt attend principally to great events, which affect mankind only at large. But the biographer may enter into the walks of private life, and exhibit characters intereſting to us as individuals. An acquaintance with hiſtory may enable a man to ſhine in converſation; but a knowledge of biography will tend more to improve the heart. Now, to render biography pleaſing, there ought to be both variety and dignity in the actions of the perſon whoſe life is recorded; without variety the reader cannot be pleaſed, and unleſs there be dignity he will be diſguſted. My ideas of dignity are not, however, confined to ſuch actions, as obtain the applauſe of the unthinking part of mankind. In my opinion, that man acts with true dignity, who performs all the kind and beneficent offices for his fellow creatures which he poſſibly can, and exerts himſelf to the very utmoſt in doing good. Many ſuch characters have exiſted, and, I hope, do ſtill exiſt; but few, I believe, if any, will be found to equal him

whoſe

whose life is contained in these sheets, and well deserves to be made known, as exhibiting a pattern fit to be proposed for general imitation.

Accounts of kings and conquerors are not very interesting to the bulk of mankind. Very few are likely to be in situations, which may call for the exercise of the caution to be learned from their errors, or to imitate those actions which rendered them illustrious. From such accounts, however, many useful lessons may be drawn, and that very important one amongst others, the duty of contentment in a lower station. Those who are a little conversant with history, will learn that dignity and power, however justly acquired, are constantly attended with numberless cares; and if injustice and tyranny, or artifice and fraud have been used to obtain them, every friend to virtue abhors or despises the hero and the prince, and learns to be happy in obscurity, and to rest satisfied though confined to the humbler duties of private and domestic life. To read of men who have distinguished themselves by their genius, their learning, and their application is very pleasing; and when these talents have been employed in the ſervice of mankind, and doing good appears to have been more their deſire than the acquiſition of fame, the honeſt and upright of every degree both love and reverence their names and memories. But to that, which, in an hiſtorical view, is their chief ornament few can aſpire.

Mr. Firmin's excellencies, though of the moſt exalted kind, were yet ſuch as all may imitate. It was not by the help of extraordinary knowledge in any art or ſcience, that he attracted high eſteem from ſo many of his contemporaries of great note and eminence; he gained honourable fame by a diligent application to buſineſs, a prevailing inclination to do good, and a ſerious attention to the precepts of our holy religion. His ſoul was caſt in a fine mould, and ever influenced by the laws and by the example of Jeſus; all the worthy diſpoſitions of his mind roſe to the higheſt degree of improvement, and in him we may ſee to what dignity and honour a tradeſman can attain, without being ever elevated above that rank.

The principal ſource of my information, with reſpect to the particulars I have related, has been a former life of

this

this worthy man, intitled *The Life of Mr. Thomas Firmin, late Citizen of London, written by one of his moſt intimate acquaintance.* The ſame was publiſhed in 1698, which was within a year after Mr. Firmin's death. Intimate acquaintance are oftentimes partial, but there is not the leaſt reaſon to doubt the truth of the leading actions of Mr. Firmin's life, ſince they were of public notoriety, are confirmed by contemporary hiſtorians, by authentic records, and have been again and again related in various biographical works of the higheſt repute and authority. The original life has been long out of print and is become ſcarce, thoſe who have ſeen it will, unleſs I am deceived, think with me, that Mr. Firmin's public ſpirited and beneficent actions may be related in a more regular, perſpicuous and ſtriking manner, than is done in the account given of them by his friend. I am at the ſame time fully convinced, that my attempt falls very ſhort of doing juſtice to the ſubject: but until a better hiſtory of Mr. Firmin's life be publiſhed, I hope that this, however imperfect, will not be entirely uſeleſs, as it may be a means of bringing ſome few at leaſt into an acquaintance with a character which deſerves to be univerſally known.

If the ſhort hiſtories which are here given of ſome eminent perſons ſhould appear, to any readers, not ſufficiently connected with the principal deſign of this work, yet I hope ſuch will not be ſevere in their cenſures. None are mentioned but thoſe with whom Mr. Firmin was particularly connected, and as his forming theſe connections redounded not a little to his honour, I thought a few particulars concerning them, however well known to the learned, might be agreeable to thoſe whoſe improvement I had principally in view when compiling this work. My own taſte may perhaps have miſled my judgment, for nothing is ſo pleaſing to me in works of any kind as anecdotes relating to perſons of diſtinguiſhed merit. I have likewiſe the authority of Dr. Birch on my ſide, whoſe life of Archbiſhop Tillotſon, which hath been very well received by the public, is remarkable for the notice therein taken of the Archbiſhop's friends. I have been alſo pretty free in making remarks and obſervations on the various incidents which I thought worthy to be recorded. Some

choose

choofe to throw remarks of this kind into notes, which I believe caufes them to be oftentimes overlooked. Others choofe to interfperfe them with the hiftory itfelf, which in my judgment is the method moft likely to imprefs, upon the minds of readers, thofe fentiments which an author fhould wifh to convey. I am moft concerned leaft they fhould be thought too numerous, or not fufficiently pertinent. Not that this is my opinion of them, if fo, it would have been folly to have publifhed them to the world; but I well know how partial a man is to his own fentiments, and his own method of writing, and therefore I fhould fubmit my judgment to that of the Public; and endeavour, as far as my knowledge and ability extended, to confult the general tafte, as to the method of conveying my ideas. To pleafe all is indeed impoffible; my higheft expectations will be anfwered, if the candid and judicious fhould regard this attempt as in fome degree worthy of their encouragement and recommendation.

Some, perhaps, may imagine that an attachment to Mr. Firmin's peculiar religious fentiments, and a defire of promoting

moting a regard to them in others, might be a principal inducement with me to republiſh his life. Such will be miſtaken, for the opinions with reſpect to our bleſſed Saviour, which Mr. Firmin eſpouſed and maintained, were different from thoſe which I have adopted and ſtill adhere to. I am, however, very free to acknowledge, that the ſincere and ardent love of truth, which appeared to reign in his breaſt, hath greatly increaſed my veneration for him, and it would be well if all would ſeek after truth with that diligence which he did, for whatever might be the reſult of their inquiries, the principle by which they were actuated would be a noble one.

I could have quoted many more authorities in ſupport of the facts which are related, but I thought it unneceſſary, ſince thoſe produced are quite ſufficient to eſtabliſh the truth of them; and it would be uſeleſs to refer to ſeveral authors, for the proof of that againſt which o one wi'l object. Whatever faults there may be in the compoſition, the reader may be aſſured that the utmoſt fidelity has been uſed in the narration, nor indeed have I been underthe leaſt

temp-

temptation to ſet off the hero of my work with borrowed ornaments. To make Mr. Firmin's character the object of general admiration, it needs only to be placed in its true light. This I have endeavoured to do, and though my attempt may incur cenſure, yet it will afford me no little conſolation, if my private ſtudies are rendered in the ſmalleſt degree ſubſervient to the intereſts of virtue and religion.

I ſhould be guilty of an unpardonable omiſſion, if I did not acknowledge my obligations, to the Rev. Dr. Kippis of London, and the Rev. Mr. Bretland of Exeter, whoſe very friendly remarks and obſervations have contributed much towards the improvement of my work. The faults which remain, are not to be imputed to either of theſe Gentlemen; but had it not been for their advice and aſſiſtance, the critical reader would have met with many more. As to the ſentiments of whatever kind, which I have advanced, my worthy and honoured friends are by no means to be thought anſwerable for them: they are both poſſeſſed of an amiable candour of mind, which diſpoſes them to ſerve any one

ſincerely

ſincerely intent on benefiting the public, whether all his ideas with reſpect to ſubjects of debate are conſonant to theirs or not. Dr. Kippis, who is excelled by no one in the knowledge of biography, encouraged me much to draw up this Life of Mr. Firmin, by declaring it to be his opinion that ſuch a publication might be very uſeful; adding, that he thought *Mr. Firmin to have been one of the beſt men that ever lived.*

CONTENTS.

CHAP. I. PAGE

Mr. Firmin's Birth and Parentage.—His behaviour in his Apprenticeship.—He marries, and lives in a very hoſpitable Manner.—Brief Accounts concerning ſome of the moſt noted amongſt his Acquaintance. 1

CHAP. II.

Mr. Firmin becomes a Widower, but ſoon marries again.—His Kindneſs to his Relations.—His uſeful Services to the Poor.—Some Account of Mr. Gouge, whoſe benevolent Scheme was purſued with great Succeſs by Mr. Firmin.—His Humanity to impriſoned Debtors.—His Care and Attention to diſtreſſed Families. 20

CHAP.

PAGE

CHAP. III.

Mr. Firmin's Attention to Christ's Church and St. Thomas's Hospitals;—to the Irish and French Refugees;—and to other Public and Private Charities.—Some Account of Bishop Compton. 59

CHAP. IV.

Mr. Firmin's undaunted Zeal in the Service of his Country as a Politician and a Patriot.—His Enmity to all kinds of Licentiousness:—his Endeavours to promote Virtue and Piety:—his strong Abhorrence of the Crime of Swearing, and the Method which he used to check this Vice in any of his Acquaintance. 85

CHAP. V.

An Account of Mr. Firmin's religious Sentiments, and of his pious Endeavours to promote what appeared to him to be the true Doctrines of the Gospel.—His great Kindness to Mr. Biddle, together with some

PAGE

Memoirs of that extraordinary Man. —The Friendſhip of Archbiſhop Tillotſon and Biſhop Fowler for Mr. Firmin, with ſome Particulars concerning theſe eminent and worthy Divines.—Other Inſtances of Mr. Firmin's Charity to the Sufferers for Religion. 101

CHAP. VI.

Mr. Firmin's Sickneſs and Death.— He is attended in his laſt Illneſs by Biſhop Fowler, of whom a ſhort Account is given.—The Reſpect paid to Mr. Firmin's Memory by Lady Clayton.—Reflections on his Character, with ſome Extracts from a Sermon preached on Occaſion of his Deceaſe. 145

ADVERTISEMENT.

THE Author lives at ſuch a diſtance from London, that he could not undertake to correct the errors of the preſs, and therefore hopes that the reader will not impute any miſtakes of this kind, if any ſuch there be, to negligence or inattention in him.

THE

LIFE

OF

MR. THOMAS FIRMIN.

CHAP. I.

Mr. Firmin's Birth and Parentage. His Behaviour in his Apprenticeship. He marries, and lives in a very hospitable Manner. Brief Accounts concerning some of the most noted amongst his Acquaintance.

MR. THOMAS FIRMIN was born at Ipſwich (a very large and populous town in the county of Suffolk), in the month of June, 1632. His parents, Henry and Prudence Firmin, as they did not abound in wealth, ſo neither were they in ſtrait or mean circumſtances *. They were in that middle ſtation, which con-

* Life, page 5, 6.

tains all that is valuable and desireable in wealth, without the temptations and dangers, to which wealth exposes men. This condition of life many persons of wisdom and experience have thought favourable to virtue above any other. The parents of the worthy man, whose life we are now entering upon, proved, at least in one instance, the justice of this remark; for on account of their sobriety, diligence, and good conduct, the effects of their piety, they were held in great esteem and reputation. They were of the number of those then called Puritans, by the loose and ignorant vulgar, who used to deem affected and precise, such as were more conscientious, devout and exemplary than ordinary, even though professed members of the Church of England.

Mr. Firmin, we may naturally suppose, was carefully instructed by his pious parents in all moral and religious duties; but, as nothing remarkable is recorded of him during the years of his childhood, we must pass on to the time, when being of a proper age he was bound apprentice to a tradesman in London *. His beha-

* Life, page 6, 7.

viour

viour in this ſituation was diligent and obliging, and he was ſo remarkably nimble in all his motions, and ſo quick and ready in taking down, opening goods, &c. that many called him "*the Spirit.*"

In making bargains, his words and manner of addreſs were ſo pleaſing and reſpectful, that afer ſome time the cuſtomers choſe rather to deal with Thomas, than with the maſter of the ſhop; and, when there happened any little diſpute about the value of a commodity, he would decide it to the ſatisfaction of both his maſter and the cuſtomer.

It would be much to the credit and advantage of all apprentices to imitate him in theſe particulars.

Nothing recommends a youth ſo much as diligence in his maſter's buſineſs, accompanied with an obliging deportment towards all thoſe who have any dealings with him. Seaſons and occaſions may alſo happen, when a young man may find it of the utmoſt ſervice to have gained the favourable opinion of thoſe with whom he is connected. Mr. Firmin met with one very diſagreeable event in the courſe of his ſervitude: the elder apprentice took five pounds of his maſter's

 money,

money, and laid it to young Firmin's charge. Whether the imputation was believed or not the friend who wrote his life was uncertain. "Probably * (says he) it was not." The reasons of this probability are very evident. If a young man be idle, sullen, and neglectful of his master's interest, any ill thing is easily believed concerning him. On the contrary, where there is any room to hope, all are ready to favour one, who recommends himself by those qualities which are proper for his station. However of Mr. Firmin's innocence in this affair no doubt remains.

The elder apprentice was shortly after this transaction seized with a mortal sickness, and before he died made confession, that it was he himself who had taken and spent the money, Mr. Firmin not having been in the least degree privy to it. Thus was his innocence made apparent to all, the consciousness of which, as may be easily supposed, was a most noble support to his own mind, whilst he lay under the charge.

Mr. Firmin, as soon as the term of his apprenticeship expired, began to trade

* Life, page 8.

for himſelf, ſetting out with the very ſmall ſtock of one hundred pounds *. But he was poſſeſſed of thoſe qualities, which are generally found to be more ſerviceable to a man than a large capital. Thoſe qualities were fidelity, induſtry, and amiable manners, which had recommended him to the love and eſteem of all thoſe who dealt with his maſter, or lived in the neighbourhood. He alſo ſtood high in the opinion of the merchants; and, having made a large acquaintance who were attached to his intereſt, purely on account of his merit, he ſpeedily overcame the difficulties, which uſually attend thoſe who enter upon buſineſs with very little money of their own. Parents and friends often make themſelves very uneaſy from an apprehenſion, that the trifling ſums, with which thoſe for whom they are concerned ſet out in life, will be entirely inadequate to their wants, and prevent them from ever riſing much above ſtraits and difficulties. But it frequently happens that this ſeeming diſadvantage, by leading a man to obſerve the neceſſity of being diligent, attentive, and obliging,

* Life, page 9.

proves the very means of advancing him; whilst those, who, depending on their own fortunes, neglect the surer methods of thriving, and disappoint the hopes which their relations had been led to form. No stock, how great soever, can render a man successful in trade, without the concurrence of those qualities, which beget confidence and respect. If a youth be of an amiable disposition, and have a turn for business, there is but little cause for anxiety as to his future welfare.

In the year 1660. Mr. Firmin married a citizen's daughter with five hundred pounds as a portion, which though not a large sum, was to him who knew so well how to improve it, a valuable acquisition.

The great expense of supporting a family in this age of dissipation and luxury renders many young traders, and indeed persons of all professions, very averse from matrimony. But it is to be hoped, that, notwithstanding the prevailing love of pleasure, there are still many amongst our fair countrywomen, who are fond of domestic life, and of all those duties which may render it comfortable and agreeable. Such a one, even

without

without a fortune, is a treaſure in herſelf, and will be more likely, upon the whole, to ſave expenſes than to increaſe them. Young men of warm paſſions are expoſed to temptations, which ſmall degrees of virtue and reſolution are not able to withſtand; and, putting religion out of the queſtion, none but the unthinking and ſuperficial would recommend the too common method of ſatisfying the ſenſual deſires. How much the health is endangered thereby all are ſenſible, and the expenſes attending ſuch a courſe have ruined thouſands. Beſides, occaſional converſe with the abandoned part of the female ſex, very frequently begets an ill opinion of every woman; ſo that thoſe who have been uſed to the company of proſtitutes, loſe all reliſh for the delicate pleaſures of virtuous love; and, if they find it convenient to marry, have ſeldom that reſpect and eſteem for a wife, which is neceſſary to render the nuptial ſtate a happy one.

In general, thoſe, who inveigh moſt warmly againſt the vanity, inconſtancy and frailty of the female ſex, have converſed pretty freely with the worſt part of them. There are but few caſes and circumſtances, in which it will not be the moſt prudent and economical way of proceeding to marry early in life; but ſhould any thing particular render this inexpedient, the wiſeſt courſe will be, to win the affections of ſome chaſte and virtuous female, to be attached ſolely to her as a lover, and, as ſoon as affairs will permit, to become her huſband. Thus will the purity of the mind and the health of the body be preſerved, the expenſes attending irregular courſes be avoided, and a fair proſpect of happineſs be ever in view as an excitement to application and diligence.

Mr. Firmin, when he became a houſe-keeper, was diſcreet and prudent, yet he practiſed in an eminent degree that good old Engliſh virtue hoſpitality. From his firſt entrance on buſineſs he ſought all opportunities of becoming acquainted with perſons of learning and worth, whether foreigners or his own country-men, and more eſpecially with miniſters *. He was ſeldom without ſome of the laſt ſort at his table, which, though attended with expenſe, anſwered, as he thought,

* Life, page 9.

very

very valuable ends. Their converſation helped to inform and enlarge his mind, and their friendſhip was of great uſe to him afterwards, in ſerving and aſſiſting the poor, which was the delight and pleaſure of his life. For having a large acquaintance, he was enabled to procure the powerful intereſt of ſome, and the liberal contributions of others, towards forwarding his important and charitable deſigns.

Mr. Firmin was ſettled in Lombard-Street, in the pariſh of St. Mary Woolnoth, the miniſters of which pariſh were firſt Mr. Samuel Jacomb and then Dr. Outram. With theſe two excellent preachers and learned men, he maintained a cloſe correſpondence. Mr. Jacomb was a divine of a free temper and genius, not confining himſelf to the ancient ſyſtems, but inclined to more liberal notions *. He died in the thirtieth year of his age; ſo that the world had not long the benefit of his labours. Now alſo it was that Mr. Firmin became intimate with thoſe very celebrated divines Whichcote, Worthington, Wilkins, and Tillotſon.

* See Birch's Life of Tillotſon, page 399.

Dr. Benjamin Whichcote was descended from an ancient and reputable family in the county of Salop; he was born in March, 1609, and in 1626 was admitted a student of Emanuel College Cambridge, of which he was elected fellow in 1633, and became a most excellent tutor. Dr. Samuel Collins, Provost of King's College in that University, being ejected by the parliament visitors, Dr. Whichcote was admitted to it in March, 1644. Dr. Collins was pleased to see a man of such learning and virtue succeed him; and Dr. Whichcote, who rather scrupled at first to accept this place, was at length prevailed upon to do it, and made it appear that his view was more to usefulness than wordly profit; for he punctually paid his predecessor half the income *. He preached a lecture for twenty years at Trinity church in Cambridge, using his utmost endeavours to promote a spirit of sober piety, and rational religion †. The happy effects of his pains appeared in the fine talents and excellent performances of so many eminent preachers after the Restoration, most of whom, and

* Biographical Dictionary.

† Tillotson's Sermon on his death.

Tillotson

Tillotſon amongſt the reſt, had received their education at Cambridge, and been formed at leaſt, if not actually brought up, by him. Others have ſince copied from, and in ſome reſpects improved upon theſe excellent models; ſo that Dr. Whichcote had the honour of leading the way to that ſolid, uſeful, practical way of preaching, which is now adopted by the learned of all parties. In the year 1662, he was choſen miniſter of St. Anne's Black-Friars, in London, where he continued till the great fire in 1666, when his church was burnt down; but ſoon after he was preſented by the Crown to the vicarage of St. Lawrence Jewry, where he continued in high reputation till his death, which happened in May, 1683, in the 73d year of his age.

Biſhop Burnet, amongſt other things greatly to his honour, ſays of him; "That "he ſet young ſtudents on conſidering "the Chriſtian Religion, as a doctrine "ſent from God, both to elevate and "ſweeten human nature, in which he "was a great example as well as a wiſe "and kind inſtructor. *" Select ſermons of

* Hiſtory of his own times, vol. I. p. 186. fol.

of Dr. Whichcote's were publiſhed in the year 1698, by the famous Earl of Shafteſbury author of the Characteriſtics. The Earl wrote an extraordinary preface to them, in which he not only ſpeaks in the higheſt terms of the Doctor, but appears in the light of a warm friend to geniune Chriſtianity, of the excellent nature and tendency of which he had formed a very high opinion *. It is to be lamented that his Lordſhip having ſuch ſentiments of the Goſpel, as he there expreſſes, ſhould have dropped any thing in his writings to depreciate the New Teſtament. But when a deſire of obtaining literary fame is the ruling paſſion, writers are ſtrongly inclined to advance what is new, even in oppoſition to what is uſeful. To this deſire may be aſcribed many of thoſe free things, which ingenious men have advanced, and the enemies of religion and virtue have been glad to lay hold of. Thoſe who are poſſeſſed of great talents, ought to be much on their guard, when writing on ſubjects of importance; for even a witticiſm may injure a good

* The preface is very curious and the whole is inſerted in the Biographical Dictionary under the article Whichcote.

cauſe,

caufe, and a jeft weighs more with moft men than folid and learned arguments.' Three other volumes of Dr. Whichcote's fermons have been publifhed, and alfo a collection of religious and moral aphorifms. They do not abound in the ornaments of ftyle; what chiefly recommends them is the excellence of their matter.

Dr. John Worthington, mafter of Jefus College in Cambridge, and preacher at St. Bennet Fink in London, died in the year 1671 at Hackney, where he had been chofen lecturer the year before. "He "was ever regarded in a moft amiable "light, as a perfect example of unwearied "diligence and activity in his profeffion, "and for the general fervice of mankind; "being furnifhed with a great ftock of all "excellent learning proper for a divine; "pious and grave, without morofenefs or "affectation, as remarkable for his humi-"lity as his knowledge; zealous in his "friendfhips; charitable beyond the pro-"portion of his eftate; univerfally inof-"fenfive, kind and obliging, even to thofe "who differed from him; not paffionate "or contentious in debates or contro-"verfies of religion; of eminent zeal for "the promotion of learning and piety, and

"indefatigable

" indefatigable in collecting, reviewing,
" and publishing, the works of Mr. Joseph
" Mede, which he did with so much
" care, that it would be hard to instance
" either in our own nation, or perhaps
" any where else, in so vast a work, that
" was ever published with more ex-
" actness; by which he raised up to him-
" self a monument likely to last as long
" as learning and religion shall continue
" in the world *."

His attention to that valuable publication, and to the duties of his profession, besides the correspondence, which he carried on with the learned, took up so much time, as to prevent him from obliging the world with much of his own; besides a volume of miscellanies published in octavo after his death, an excellent catechism is commonly ascribed to him. This was drawn up wholly in the words of Scripture, and not in the phrases peculiar to any party of Christians; for he was (to use Bp. Fowler's expression) "a great " enemy to man-made divinity." And surely the doctrines and duties of the Gospel, cannot be better expressed than in

* Birch's life of Tillotson, page 377.

the words of the inſpired writers. The more theſe are adhered to, the more will peace and holineſs prevail. Thoſe have ever been in all ages of the church the moſt amiable and uſeful men, who have endeavoured in every thing to conform, as nearly as poſſible, to the great ſtandard of truth.

Dr. John Wilkins, another of Mr. Firmin's learned friends, was born in 1614, near Daventry in Northamptonſhire. His grandfather by the mother's ſide, was the good Mr. Dod, well known for his ſayings, and diſtinguiſhed likewiſe by the ſufferings * which he patiently endured, for refuſing a compliance with the many ceremonies, which Archbiſhop Laud and others endeavoured, with a popiſh zeal, to introduce into the Church of England. Dr. Wilkins was ſuch a proficient in claſſical learning, that, at the age of 13 †, he was entered a ſtudent at New College in Oxford. In 1656, he married the ſiſter of Oliver Cromwell, and was preferred to the maſterſhip of Trinity College

* Neal's Hiſtory of the Puritans.

† Life of Biſhop Wilkin's, prefixed to ſome of his Works, publiſhed in Oct. 1708.

in Cambridge by Richard Cromwell in the year 1659, which office he held but for a ſhort time, being ejected upon the Reſtoration. He was not favourably thought of at the court of Charles II. on account of his connection with the Protector's family; and being alſo very enlarged as to his religious ſentiments, and deſirous of uniting all parties together by mutual conceſſions, his preferment in the church was oppoſed by Archbiſhop Sheldon, whoſe influence was great *. The Duke of Buckingham however ſo effectually recommended him to the king, that he was advanced to the ſee of Cheſter in 1668, which high dignity he enjoyed but a ſhort time, dying of the ſtone in 1672.

Biſhop Wilkins was not only a great divine, but alſo a very eminent philoſopher. He was one of the firſt members of the Royal Society, and indefatigable in promoting every kind of uſeful knowledge. All his writings were ingenious and learned, and many of them very curious and entertaining; and he ſtands amongſt the foremoſt of thoſe, from

* Burnet's Hiſtory of his Own Times, vol. I. p. 253.

whoſe

whoſe ſtudies the world has received immenſe benefit. The learned of all profeſſions loved him; and, what is more, the greateſt and beſt qualities are aſcribed to him, by ſo many eminent and good men, that he will be one of the illuſtrious few, whom the moſt diſtant times and ages will revere *.

Dr. Tillotſon, that great and amiable divine, at the time of Mr. Firmin's firſt acquaintance with him, preached the Tueſday lecture at St. Lawrence Jewry, then ſo much frequented by all the divines of the town, and by a great many perſons of quality and diſtinction. When obliged to be out of London, as he frequently was, either on buſineſs or for relaxation or health, he generally left it to Mr. Firmin to provide preachers for his lecture †; and he fulfilled this truſt ſo well that there was never any complaint on account of Dr. Tillotſon's abſence, ſome eminent divine always appearing in his room. Mr. Firmin was very fit to undertake this ſervice, for now there was hardly a clergyman of

* For teſtimonies in proof of his uncommon worth, ſee his article in the Biographical Dictionary.

† Mr. Firmin's Life, p. 14.

note,

note, that lived in or frequented London, with whom he was not become acquainted. This circumſtance enabled him to render material ſervice to many hopeful young preachers and ſcholars, the candidates for ſchools, lectures, curacies, or rectories, for whom he would ſolicit with as much affection and diligence as other perſons are wont to do for relations and children.

See here a tradeſman, who underſtood neither Latin nor Greek, logic or philoſophy, honoured with the intimacy and friendſhip of the moſt learned and eminent perſons of the age, and who notwithſtanding differed widely from him in opinion as to religious matters, and were continually attacking his ſuppoſed errors of doctrine. But as the clearneſs of his natural underſtanding, joined to an uncommon ſolidity of judgment, enabled him to refute their arguments, at leaſt to his own ſatisfaction; ſo his ſteadineſs in maintaining what he believed to be the truth did not leſſen their regard for him. This is one proof amongſt many others, that the wideſt differences in religious ſentiments will never ſet good men at variance, if their natural tempers

be-

be amiable, and they be disposed to allow one another the same liberty of thinking and judging, which each claims for himself. What Mr. Firmin's religious sentiments were, or rather what were his endeavours to propagate them from a conviction of their truth and importance, is a matter worth knowing. But his great and extensive charities claim our first attention, and will create a warm love for him in the breast of very benevolent reader. Such a one no doubt, if a stranger to his character before, now begins to reverence it; for if a man may be known by the company he keeps, Mr. Firmin must certainly have been a most excellent person.

CHAP.

CHAP. II.

Mr. Firmin becomes a Widower, but ſoon marries again. His Kindneſs to his Relations. His uſeful Services to the Poor. Some Account of Mr. Gouge, whoſe benevolent Scheme was purſued with great Succeſs by Mr. Firmin. His Humanity to impriſoned Debtors. His Care and Attention to diſtreſſed Families.

MR. FIRMIN had been married but a ſhort time, when death deprived him of his wife. She had brought him two children, a ſon and a daughter, the former of whom lived to man's eſtate, bnt died a bachelor about ſeven years before his father. Biographers have taken notice of what they call a very remarkable circumſtance with regard to Mrs. Firmin's death, in which many will think, and perhaps very juſtly, that there was nothing at all extraordinary. "Mr. "Firmin, it ſeems, being at Cambridge, "dreamed that he ſaw his wife breath-"ing her laſt: whereupon he took horſe

"early

" early in the morning for London, and " on the way thither, he met the meſſen- " ger who was ſent to give him notice " of her deceaſe *." God may, without doubt, in the courſe of his wiſe providence, ſee fit, in dreams and viſions of the night, or when men are engaged in their common buſineſs, to ſuggeſt ſuch thoughts to their minds, as may be a means of doing them real ſervice. But as it does not appear that any wiſe or good end could be anſwered by this dream, as his wife was dead before he could poſſibly come to her aſſiſtance, ought it not to be aſcribed to thoſe fancies of the brain of which no rational account has been yet given. The laying any ſtreſs upon dreams, unleſs evidently calculated to anſwer ſome valuable purpoſe, only ſerves to prop up the old rotten cauſe of ſuperſtition, every degree of which may prove a ſource of uneaſineſs to ſome honeſt and good minds.

Mr. Firmin, having experienced the comforts of the married ſtate, did not remain very long without another partner,

* Life, p. 11. All thoſe who have written Mr. Firmin's life in Dictionaries, &c. have thought fit to retain this trifling anecdote.

but

but as ſoon as it was decent, paid his addreſſes to the daughter of a juſtice of the peace in the county of Eſſex *. He had with this lady, who poſſeſſed all the qualifications of a good wife, a very conſiderable portion. God was pleaſed to lend them ſeveral children. It may properly be ſaid *lend*, for but one of them lived to man's eſtate, who was named Giles. His father gave him the whole portion which his mother had brought, and he was likely to become a reſpectable merchant, but he died, when juſt about to embark for Portugal, where his buſineſs called for his preſence.

Mr. Firmin's firſt matrimonial connection was diſſolved in leſs than four years: as to the continuance of the ſecond, which commenced in 1664, no particular mention is made in any of the accounts relating to him, and authors have alſo been ſilent as to his character in the domeſtic relations of a father and a huſband. That he filled up theſe important relations in a becoming manner we have ſufficient reaſon to believe from the whole tenor of his conduct, which

* Life, page 26.

was

was ſuch as to leave no room for the ſuſpicion of negligence in any of the duties incumbent on him. It is more eſpecially very worthy of being obſerved, that, when he was poſſeſſed of but a moderate capital, and his manner of living was attended with conſiderable expenſe, neither of theſe circumſtances, nor that of his having an increaſing family prevented him from being a moſt kind brother, uncle and kinſman *.

There are too many of thoſe, whom the world ſtyles good ſort of people, whoſe cares center entirely in themſelves, and their very neareſt connections; but true generoſity enlarges the heart. What St. Paul ſays to Timothy (as it is well rendered in the margin of our Bibles;) "He that provides not for his own "kindred is worſe than an infidel †." was religiouſly attended to by Mr. Firmin. His loſſes by ſome of his relations, for whom he had advanced money, and his diſburſements for others amounted to very conſiderable ſums, and moſt of thoſe loſſes happened to him juſt after his entering upon buſineſs. But he was diſpoſed to

* Life, p. 12. † 1 Tim. v. 8.

improve

improve the present hour, aud not to defer all his acts of kindness and liberality till he had an abundance. He always kept his heart open, and never appears to have formed a design of amassing any particular sum, the aiming at which has been a means of contracting and hardening the hearts of numbers. All should accustom themselves, according to their ability, to do liberal and kind things frequently, and then in all probability their benevolent dispositions will increase with their riches. This was Mr. Firmin's method, and though his knowledge of and diligence in business, would soon have acquired him a very large fortune, yet, when he arrived to the 44th year of his age *, he was worth only about nine thousand pounds, which was more by half than he left behind him at his decease †, though he might have increased his wealth daily. But so far was avarice from growing upon him with years, that he became more and more indifferent to the world the longer he lived in it; though he had always that commendable degree of prudence, which

* Life, p. 28. † Life, p. 38.

rendered

rendered him ſo far attentive to his own intereſt, as not only to keep himſelf out of all difficulties, but to be enabled alſo to be doing good to the very laſt.

The year 1665 is remarkable in the Engliſh annals for a great plague, of which there died in London only, though perhaps not more than half ſo populous as at preſent, one hundred thouſand perſons *. Moſt of the wealthy citizens removed themſelves and their families into the country, and ſo did Mr. Firmin, but he left a kinſman in his houſe (ſince it was neceſſary that ſome one ſhould be there) with orders to relieve certain of the poor weekly, and to give them out ſtuff to employ them in making their uſual commodities. He foreſaw that he ſhould be hard put to it to diſpoſe of the large quantities, which thoſe poor people would work off in ſo long a time for him only; but he truſted to the providence of the Father of mercies, who we may be ſure, obſerved with pleaſure and approbation ſuch an inſtance of compaſſion and tenderneſs. His expectations of being ſome how or other aſſiſted in the diſpoſal

* See all the Hiſtories of that Time.

of this great ſtock were not diſappointed. On his return to London, a wealthy chapman, who was much pleaſed with this uſeful and adventurous charity, made an extraordinary purchaſe of theſe goods, and by that means Mr. Firmin avoided any loſs by then employing the poor *.

The plague was followed, the next year, by that dreadful fire, which laid almoſt the whole city of London in aſhes, the churches and public buildings, as well as the habitations of the poor and the rich being involved in one common ruin. Mr. Firmin's houſe in Lombard Street was burned in that great conflagration, but he immediately took another, with a warehouſe belonging to it, in Leaden-Hall-Street. In this he was fortunate above many others, ſince few could be accommodated with houſes, the fire having ſpared but a comparatively ſmall number, which had been occupied before this diſtreſſing event happened. Moſt perſons were therefore obliged to confine themſelves to ſtrait lodgings, and loſe the benefit of their trades, till the

* Life, page 27.

immenſe

immenſe heaps of rubbiſh were cleared away, and new buildings raiſed in the places of the old.

Mr. Firmin was now become a perſon of note, his noble ſpirit and generous way of trading having greatly recommended him; and in a few years he ſo improved his ſtock, as to be able to rebuild his own houſe, and almoſt the whole of the court in which he lived. As ſoon as he had performed this duty to himſelf and his family, he began to build for the benefit of the poor; for whoſe ſervice he erected a warehouſe near the banks of the river Thames*. In this, corn and coals were laid up, to be ſold in dear ſeaſons at a moderate price, that was never to exceed their firſt coſt, unleſs the ſtores were any way damaged by keeping; in that caſe, the loſs was to be made up by ſelling the reſt at a higher rate. This was a very uſeful charity, and of much ſervice to the objects of it, ſince it prevented them from feeling the inconveniences of dearth, which muſt ever be attended with want, when families are large, and the wages only ſufficient

* Life, page 28.

 for

for a bare ſupport at cheaper times. Beſides being at the trouble of attending to this buſineſs, which was not ſmall, it does not appear that Mr. Firmin made any account of the expenſe he had been at in building, or of the intereſt of his money which at that time was conſiderable, 8 per cent. being common, and even 10 being to be had on reaſonable ſecurity.

Mr. Firmin very wiſely judged that no charity could be ſo ſerviceable to the poor, as that which kept them out of idleneſs, and therefore in the year 1676, (at which time it was that his capital amounted to about nine thouſand pounds) he did the moſt eminent ſervice both to them and the public, by erecting a warehouſe in Little-Britain near Smithfield, for the employment of the needy and induſtrious in the linen manufacture*. Dr. Tillotſon mentioned this deſign with great approbation in his funeral ſermon for Mr. Gouge, preached in 1681, which ſermon is preſerved amongſt the other works of that celebrated prelate.

* Life, page 29.

" He (Mr. Gouge) ſet the poor of " St. Sepulchre's pariſh, of which he was " miniſter, to work at his own charge. " He bought flax and hemp for them to " ſpin; when ſpun, he paid them for their " work, and cauſed it to be wrought into " cloth, which he ſold as he could, him- " ſelf bearing the whole loſs. This was a " very wiſe and well choſen way of cha- " rity, and in the good effects of it a much " greater charity than if he had given " to thoſe very perſons freely, and for " nothing, ſo much as he made them " earn by their work: becauſe by this " means he reſcued them from two moſt " dangerous temptations, idleneſs and " poverty.

" This courſe ſo happily deviſed and " begun by Mr. Gouge, gave, it may be, " the firſt hint to that uſeful and worthy " citizen Mr. Thomas Firmin, of a much " larger deſign, which has been managed " by him ſome years in this city with " that vigour and good ſucceſs, that " many hundreds of poor children and " others who lived idle before, unpro- " fitable both to themſelves and the " public, now maintain themſelves, and " are alſo ſome advantage to the commu-

 " nity.

" nity. By the affiftance and charity of " many excellent and well difpofed " perfons, Mr. Firmin is enabled to bear " the unavoidable lofs and charge of fo " vaft an undertaking; and by his own " forward inclination to charity, and un- " wearied diligence and activity, is fitted " to fuftain and go through the incre- " dible pains of it."

Mr. Gouge was a man moft eminent for piety and ufefulnefs, and in the temper and difpofition of his mind greatly refembled Mr. Firmin, who highly efteemed him, and prevailed on him to live at his houfe *. Never did one houfe contain two perfons of fuch different ages and profeffions, whofe fouls were more nearly allied. Both their hearts were warmed with benevolence and love, and their mutual friendfhip could not fail of cherifhing thofe divine principles. Mr. Firmin, being the youngeft by almoft thirty years, muft have derived great benefit from fuch a connection; and his activity and zeal undoubtedly afforded the higheft fatisfaction to Mr. Gouge, who could with pleafure devife methods

* Life, page 49.

of

of doing good, when he found another ſo ready to execute them. All that one man could do, he himſelf did; and, to his unſpeakable pleaſure, he met with another ready to adopt and purſue every charitable ſcheme, which he, whoſe whole attention was directed to the ſervice of his fellow creatures, could point out. To recount all his benevolent labours would require a volume; but a brief memorial may ſerve to give us ſome ideas of his excellencies, whom Mr. Firmin moſt gladly choſe to be a fellow inhabitant of his manſion.

Mr. Gouge was born in the year 1604, at Bow in Middleſex, and received his ſchool education at Eton, and his univerſity learning at Oxford. He left the univerſity and his fellowſhip, for the living of Colſden in Surry, where he had not been long, before he was removed to the large and populous pariſh of St. Sepulchre's in London; of which he was, for twenty-four years, a moſt diligent and faithful miniſter. He was unwearied in the laborious duties of conſtant preaching, viſiting the ſick, and catechizing in the church all who would come. To encourage the poor (who were generally the most ignorant) to seek for instruction, he distributed money amongst them once a-week, changing the day that they might be obliged constantly to attend. As for the poor who were able to get their own living, he set them to work, buying flax and hemp for them to spin, which when manufactured he sold as he could amongst his friends.

The Bartholomew act obliged him to quit his living in 1662 *; for he was dissatisfied with the terms of conformity then imposed. This was a great loss to his parish and also to himself, as the living was a very valuable one; but as he had then a good estate, his charity to the poor was continued. He made it the great business of his life to serve them, and applied himself to it with as much constancy and diligence, as other men do to their trades. He suffered much by the fire of London, and this, together with settling his children, reduced his income to one hundred and fifty pounds yearly. Of this he always spent one hundred in works of charity, urging others to assist him in his benevolent designs, though it

* Nonconformist's Memorial, last edition, p. 144.

does

does not appear, that he perſuaded any to do ſo largely as himſelf.

Beſides employing the poor, he was much ſet on inſtructing them in religion, well knowing from his own experience, that piety is the foundation on which all other virtues muſt be built. And in that he judged rightly. For certainly thoſe are moſt likely to ſubmit to the evils of life with patience, and to fulfil the duties of it amidſt temptations and ſnares, who have a firm faith in, and a good hope towards God, as the bountiful and powerful rewarder of all thoſe who diligently ſeek his favour, by yielding a willing obedience to his commands. To promote theſe valuable ends, he freely gave to the poor ſuch books as *The Whole Duty of Man*, *The Practice of Piety*, and others of the like kind, containing ſuch things only as good chriſtians are agreed in, and not matters of doubtful diſputation. Theſe he cauſed to be printed in Welch, and his ſpirit was ſo far from partaking of narrowneſs or bigotry, that he procured the *Church Catechiſm* with a practical expoſition of it, and alſo the *Common Prayer* to be printed likewiſe in that language, and given to ſuch as would otherwiſe have been unable to get them. It has however been inſinuated, that his charities in Wales, were deſigned only to ſerve a party, and that the diſſenters have increaſed in conſequence of them *. If this be the caſe, it muſt be purely owing to the increaſe of piety, for Mr. Gouge never gave the people a ſingle book, nor can be charged with having uſed a ſingle argument to perſuade them to nonconformity. Indeed no one can wonder, who conſiders by what wretched and deſpicable hirelings the Welch churches are frequently ſerved, that teachers of any denomination, who appear to have ſome degree of zeal and ſeriouſneſs, ſhould be attended to and followed. Until the eſtabliſhed clergy of that principality pay more regard to their duty, than has hitherto been cuſtomary amongſt them †, all thoſe, whoſe views are ſuperior to the intereſts of any particular party, will rejoice that there are preachers of any perſuaſion, labouring to inſtruct a neglected people in the principles of our common chriſtianity, and

* Mr. Wynne's edition of Powel's Hiſtory of Wales.

† See View of the State of Religion in the dioceſe of St. David's, written by D. D. of that principality.

ardently

ardently join in the wiſhing that another Mr. Gouge may ariſe and help them.

In the latter part of his life, he confined his ſervices chiefly to that country, where he thought they were moſt wanted. Beſides diſtributing books, having obtained a licence from ſome of the biſhops to preach in Wales, he took an annual journey thither, and when more than ſixty years of age, uſed to travel about, diſtributing his charities, inſtructing the ignorant, and ſettling ſchools in the chief towns, to the number of three or four hundred; where women were employed to teach children to read, and books provided for them gratis, or ſold at a ſmall price. He uſed often to ſay with pleaſure, "that he had two livings "which he would not exchange for the "greateſt in England; viz Chriſt's Hoſ"pital, where he uſed frequently to cate"chize the poor children, and Wales, "where he went ſometimes twice in a "year to ſpread knowledge, piety, and "charity." He was ever ready to embrace and oblige all men, and if they did but fear God and work righteouſneſs, he heartily loved them, how different ſoever from him in judgment about things leſs neceſſary,

neceſſary, and even in opinions that he held very dear. But neither his excellent temper, nor the eminent ſervice he was continually doing could preſerve him in perfect tranquillity. He was perſecuted to ſuch a degree even in Wales, as to be excommunicated for preaching occaſionally, notwithſtanding he had a licence, and went conſtantly to the pariſh churches, and to the Lord's ſupper when adminiſtered in them. Yet this wicked oppoſition did not diſhearten him. He ſtill went about doing good, and was ſpared for the benefit of mankind till October 1681, when he made a peaceful and happy end, dying ſuddenly in his ſleep, being then ſeventy-ſeven years old.

Dr. Tillotſon honoured him with a funeral ſermon, in which moſt of the abovementioned particulars are recorded; and he ſpoke of his excellencies in that warm ſtyle of approbation, which became a truly Chriſtian Divine. Indeed he had a fine ſubject for panegyric; Mr. Gouge being a man in whom none but zealots could find matter for cenſure; nor had ſuch, ſays Mr. Baxter, any thing to allege againſt him, but his "not conforming entirely to their impoſitions."

In

In ſome of Mr. Gouge's uſeful charities, Mr. Firmin aſſiſted him, eſpecially in printing his edition of the Welch Bible, which was a very expenſive undertaking. To this good work, Dr. Tillotſon contributed no leſs than fifty pounds *. Mr. Firmin alſo adopted Mr. Gouge's uſeful plan, for relieving want, and at the ſame time encouraging induſtry. Of his endeavours in this way, he thus ſpeaks in a book which he wrote, intitled, *Propoſals for the Employment of the Poor.*

" It is now about four years ſince I
" ſet up my workhouſe in Little-Britain,
" for the employment of the poor in the
" linen manufacture, which hath afford-
" ed ſo great help and relief to many
" hundreds of poor families; that I never
" did, and fear I never ſhall do an action
" more to my own ſatisfaction, or to the
" good and benefit of the poor."

The late reverend and ingenious Mr. Harte, in his eſſays on huſbandry; page 156, recommends this ſcarce and valuable treatiſe of Mr. Firmin's to all the lovers of national œconomy. It contains (as Mr. Harte

* Life, page 50.

thinks)

thinks) many ufeful hints and obfervations deferving of attention; and in fome things his plan hath been followed. The public, as Mr. Harte obferves, are particularly indebted to Mr. Firmin, not only for the idea, but the actual introduction of parifh workhoufes for the more profitable employment of the half-difabled and indigent, or fuch as are too young or too old for the bufinefs of agriculture. Workhoufes indeed, owing to bad management are oftentimes wretched habitations; but if properly regulated, would conduce much to the comfort and advantage of the poor. He employed in the manufacture, which he had with fo much benevolence and difcretion eftablifhed, fixteen or feventeen hundred fpinners at a time, befides dreffers of of flax, weavers, and others *. The greateft part of thefe could not earn more than fixpence in a day, though they worked fixteen hours. Provifions were then confiderably cheaper than at prefent, but Mr. Firmin did not think their wages a fufficient recompence for their labour; on which account he was very

* Life, page 31.

liberal to them in his charities, eſpecially at chriſtmas, and in ſevere weather, and ſo attentive was he with reſpect to every thing which might contribute to their convenience and comfort, that obſerving how much they were ſoiled by carrying away coals in their aprons, and in the ſkirts of their coats, he provided canvaſs bags and gave them, that ſo there might be no circumſtance to leſſen the value of his charity.

He was perſuaded that nothing conduces more to health than cleanlineſs, and that to keep perſons clean, proper changes of linen were very requiſite and neceſſary; becauſe linen can be frequently waſhed. The poor ſpun much of this of a ſtrong coarſe ſort, and Mr. Firmin, with the aſſiſtance of his friends, would ſometimes give away fifteen hundred ſhirts and ſhifts in a year; ſo that thoſe had it in their power always to appear ſomewhat decent, who would take any tolerable care of their woollen garments. They were alſo encouraged in their labours, by perſons of fortune, whom their kind employer would perſuade to come, and be eye-witneſſes of their poverty and diligence. Such as were diſpoſed to learn the art of ſpinning had teachers hired for them; and, if any were not able to purchaſe wheels and reels for ſpinning, thoſe were bought and freely given to them. Mr. Firmin would often take up poor children as they were begging in the ſtreets, and have them taught at his own charge, providing them with things neceſſary for ſetting them to work; but never deducting any part of the coſt out of their wages *.

He reckoned himſelf fortunate, that in one year, in which he had laid out four thouſand pounds, two hundred only were loſt. This moſt would think a very conſiderable ſum to be ſunk in one mode of charity, to which ſo much time and pains were alſo devoted. The loſs however muſt have been greater, had not many perſons taken off large quantities of theſe commodities on purpoſe to encourage ſo good a work. The Eaſt-India and Guinea companies in particular bought their canvaſs of him, for pepper bags, and other coarſe merchandize, which before, they were ſupplied with from

* Life, page 32.

foreign countries. When this trade had been carried on for more than five years, at the expenſe of a thouſand pounds and upwards, Mr. Firmin publiſhed *a Book of Propoſals* to engage others to ſet the poor on working at the public charge; or at leaſt to aſſiſt him and two or three friends more. But neither the arguments which he offered in this book, nor ſuch as he urged in frequent converſations with the lord mayor, the aldermen and other wealthy citizens, could prevail upon them to concur with his benevolent deſigns; ſo that he was obliged to leſſen the ſpinning trade *.

In the year 1682, the whole diſburſement was two thouſand three hundred and thirty-ſeven pounds, two hundred and fourteen pounds of which were quite loſt. And notwithſtanding this charity was of ſo manifeſt advantage to the community, yet the loſs increaſed annually, there not being a ſufficient number of perſons to be found, who would buy the manufactures at the price they coſt him. The deficiency upon all the work of the poor, for ſeven or eight years together,

* Life, page 33.

was no lefs than twopence upon every fhilling ; but Mr. Firmin was content, and ufed to fay " two pence given them " by lofs in their work, was twice fo " much faved to the Public, in that it " took them off from beggary or theft*." But the lofs in fome years was extraordinary. In the year 1683, though the trade increafed a little, his own difburfements and thofe of his friends, were not lefs than two thoufand pounds, and the lofs four hundred. In the year 1684, the balance not then received, amounted to feven hundred and fixty-three pounds; and in the year 1685, it was increafed to nine hundred pounds. To make up for this lofs, an eminent citizen, who had five hundred pounds in that ftock, quitted the whole principal, and required no intereft †. In the following years the trade ftill declined for want of more benefactors, till the year 1690, when the defign was taken up by the Patentees of the linen manufacture, who agreed with Mr. Firmin to give him one hundred pounds per an. to overfee and govern it. But this undertaking not anfwering his expectations, or thofe of the

* Life, page. 34. † ibid.

Patentees,

Patentees, he never received the promiſed ſalary, which was a loſs to the neceſſitous labourers, to whom he would in all probability have given the whole; for he never wiſhed to derive any profit to himſelf from their induſtry: on the contrary, he loſt upwards of five hundred pounds by employing them. Once he drew ſome prizes in a lottery, to the amount of one hundred and eighty pounds, but he reſerved only the money he had riſked, and gave away the reſt; a part to ſome relations, and the remainder to the poor *.

The ſpinners being thus deſerted, Mr. Firmin returned to the care of them again, and managed the trade as before, endeavouring to make it bear its own charges, and ſupplying the deficiency of their ſmall earnings by larger contributions of charity than uſual; he beſides made applications in their behalf to perſons of all ranks, with whom he had any intimacy or friendſhip. He would even carry the cloth to thoſe with whom he had ſcarcely any acquaintance, telling them "It was the poors' cloth, which in con-
"ſcience they ought to buy at the price for

* Life, page 35.

"which it could be afforded." If the buyers were very wealthy, he would perſuade them to give ſome of what they had purchaſed towards clothing the labourers; and he took care alſo to be ſoon paid for what was ſold. Without uſing ſuch methods, he could not poſſibly have employed ſo great a number of people, who always wanted their money immediately on the delivery of their work. This continued to be his chief buſineſs and care till the day of his death, ſaving that, when the calling in of the clipped money occaſioned ſuch a ſcarcity of current coin, that many of the rich had not enough to ſend their ſervants with to market, he was forced to diſmiſs ſome of his ſpinners merely through the want of caſh to pay them. He continued to take out of the general ſtock, to the amount of ſeven hundred pounds, till Mr. James, his partner and kinſman, told him he ſhould take out no more. This was not owing to that gentleman's diſapprobation of the workhouſe charity; (on the contrary he encouraged, promoted, and freely lent money to it) but as the whole common trade went through his hands, and was managed by him, he was

was more ſenſible than Mr. Firmin, that a larger ſum of ready money could not be ſpared for that uſe, without doing a material injury to them in other reſpects *.

Flax and tow being very combuſtible goods, Mr. Firmin was always al ittle uneaſy, leaſt by ſome accident or other the workhouſe, which was in the keeping of ſervants, ſhould take fire, and a ſquib was once flung by ſome careleſs boy into the cellar, where thoſe materials were ſtored, but providentially did no harm. Concerning the workhouſe and the ſpinners, Mr Firmin would often ſay, "that to pay the labourers, to relieve them "with the money begged for them, and "with coals, garments, &c. was to him "ſuch a pleaſure, as magnificent buildings, "pleaſant walks, well cultivated orchards "and gardens, the jollity of muſic and "wine, or the charms of love or ſtudy, "are to others." In this he ſaid no more than the truth, for it appeared, on carefully examining his accounts, that he might have left a fortune behind him of at leaſt twenty thouſand pounds, if he had

* Life, pages 36, 37.

not employed moſt of his gettings in private and public charities, which ſo reduced his ſubſtance, that he died worth little more than a ſixth part of that ſum *. How glorious muſt be his reward, who was thus rich in good works, and continually laying up in ſtore for himſelf a treaſure in heaven! to this bleſſed ſtate his views were ever directed; and as to this world, it was his ſettled reſolution to quit it in very moderate circumſtances. He ſaid to a friend but a ſhort time before his deceaſe; "were I now worth forty "thouſand pounds, I ſhould leave behind "me but very little of it." It is even likely that he would have died worth leſs than he really did; for, had he come into the poſſeſſion of any large ſum, it would have engaged him in ſuch vaſt deſigns for the benefit of the poor, that he would probably have gone beyond the expenſe at firſt intended. His phyſician uſed to blame him, becauſe he did not allow himſelf a competent time for his dinner, but haſtened away to Garraway's coffee-houſe about ſuch affairs as he had taken in hand. Theſe affairs were

* Life, page 38.

ſeldom or never his own. He was either employed in ſoliciting for the poor, or doing the buſineſs of ſome friend who wanted his intereſt, or attending thoſe meetings which were held to conſult the public good. It was of vaſt advantage to him, in the diſcharge of theſe many and important concerns, that he was always very expeditious in his diſpatches, being quick above moſt men in apprehending, ſpeaking, judging, reſolving, and acting *. This natural fitneſs for buſineſs was greatly improved by a readineſs and zeal, which prompted him to the moſt vigorous exertions, whenever he could be uſeful. That was a pleaſure to him, which to perſons of a ſmaller degree of benevolence would have been a toilſome labour.

Mr. Firmin's known readineſs to engage in every undertaking, by which any good might be done, led ſome well diſpoſed perſons to perſuade him to ſet up the woollen manufacture; becauſe at this the poor could earn better wages than at the linen one, which he thought a ſufficient inducement to make the trial; and ac-

* Life, page 39.

cordingly he took a houſe for this purpoſe in Artillery Lane. But the price of wool advancing very much, and the London ſpinners, not being at all ſkilful in drawing a woollen thread, after a conſiderable loſs by them, and twenty-nine months trial he gave over the project *.

Such were the methods which he took to preſerve his fellow creatures from diſtreſs. He ſhewed equal humanity and compaſſion to ſuch as were involved in it. He was particularly zealous and active in redeeming poor debtors out of priſon, not only out of regard to their perſons, but alſo to the ſituation of their unhappy and ſtarving families. By his own liberality, added to his diligence in procuring the charitable aſſiſtance of ſeveral worthy perſons, hundreds of unfortunate creatures obtained their liberty, who were held in durance only for the fees of jailors, or very ſmall debts †. The unrelenting cruelty of ſome creditors is indeed ſhocking to humanity. The extravagant and knaviſh, without doubt, deſerve puniſhment; but to detain

* Life, page. 40. † ibid.

those whom losses or sickness, or want of ability to carry on trade with success has reduced to straits, is a most detestable practice. Did the punishment affect the unhappy debtor alone, it would be exceedingly severe. To be confined within the narrow bounds of a prison, denied the benefit of wholesome air, made a companion of the most abandoned and profligate of mankind; to be excluded from the means of rising into credit, of recovering a lost character, and becoming once more useful to society; all these circumstances render a prison dreadful to one of the least degree of sensibility. But it is impossible to conceive how exquisite must be his distress, who has a fond wife struggling with extreme indigence, and a family of innocent babes weeping for want of their daily bread. When such fall under the iron hand of oppression, what divine pleasure must that man enjoy, whose generous heart disposes him to pity and to raise them up.

Mr. Firmin, besides endeavouring to obtain the discharge of prisoners, took care also for the better and easier subsistence of those whom he could not release. He would examine them concerning the usage they had from their keepers; and he sometimes prosecuted jailors for extorting unlawful fees, and making other unreasonable demands. One jailor dreading the issue of an examination hanged himself. If from time to time some public spirited persons would look into the state of our jails, many shocking abuses might be prevented. To prevent and punish such abuses, a number of benevolent gentlemen formed themselves into a committee in the year 1729, whose praises are recorded in the immortal writings of our amiable poet Thomson *. A bard like him would find a noble subject for praise in Mr. Howard, a gentleman of Bedfordshire, who hath lately been at great expense and trouble to examine personally into the state of the prisons throughout this and the neighbouring kingdoms and states, with no other view but the generous one of alleviating the distresses of the forlorn and miserable. The author of this life, though an entire stranger to Mr. Howard, could not resist the strong inclination

* Winter, line 380——389.

which he felt of paying this ſmall tribute of reſpect to his diſintereſted goodneſs.

Mr. Firmin continued to be the friend and reliever of poor debtors, from before the year 1681, to his laſt breath; and being grieved that he could not in his private capacity, procure the releaſe of thoſe unfortunate perſons, the payment of whoſe debts was beyond the reach of common charity, he vigorouſly promoted *Acts of Grace*, by which the inſolvent might obtain a parliamentary diſcharge. He himſelf was never one of the national repreſentatives, yet he had a mighty intereſt in both houſes, and was the cauſe that many bills were withdrawn and others paſſed. That he had ſuch great influence was ſo well known, that once, when an Act of Grace for poor priſoners (which was liable to be, and was actually abuſed by unconſcionable and knaviſh people) paſſed both the houſes and obtained the Royal aſſent, he was upbraided with it by ſome of the creditors, and told it was his *Act* *.

He was not inſenſible that ſometimes people grow poor and get into priſons,

* Life, page 41.

by being negligent, idle, proud, and intemperate; yet he could not agree with thoſe who had no compaſſion for ſuch, and who would ſay, that the extravagant and vicious ought to feel the ſad conſequences of their own folly. He was wont to anſwer to ſuch reaſonings "That it "would be a miſerable world indeed, if "the Divine Providence ſhould act by "that rule; if God ſhould ſhew no "favour, grant no help or deliverance "to us, in thoſe ſtraits or calamities that "are the effect of our own ſins. If the "univerſal Lord ſeeks to reclaim and to "better us by favours and graces, do we "dare to argue againſt the example ſet "by him, and a method without which "no man living may aſk any thing of "God * ?"

Theſe were ſentiments worthy of a true chriſtian! ſome indeed are ſo bad, that nothing but ſeverity will reſtrain them from doing irreparable injury to ſociety, the ſafety of which every man ought to make the chief object of his attention. Yet to ſhew mercy and to forgive will be ever amiable, even when it

* Life, page 42.

degenerates

degenerates into weakneſs, as it certainly does when it ſuffers every bad man to go unpuniſhed. No exact rules can be laid down as to the degree in which offenders ſhould be proſecuted: men muſt be determined by their own judgements and feelings.

Poor of one ſort or another there will always be, and the number muſt be greatly increaſed in a time of dearth, ſickneſs, or decay of trade; which evils, though they be but temporary, muſt yet be ſeverely felt by thoſe, who having little or nothing to begin the world with, are broken down by ſmall loſſes. When ſuch as muſt live by the labour of their hands, enter into the married ſtate, rigid œconomiſts will blame them. Such, charge ſervants in particular with imprudence, whoſe wages will do little more than to find them in cloaths, when leaving a good place they take upon them a load of domeſtic cares. It is however well for ſociety, that the dictates of nature ſpeak louder in ſome than thoſe of quiet and eaſe. If none were ever coupled together, but ſuch as have an almoſt certain proſpect of living without want or

 anxiety,

anxiety, the next century would find our part of the world but thinly inhabited.

Mr. Firmin well knew how much thofe muft fuffer, who have large families and fmall means, and for fuch, during feveral years of his life, he begged to the amount of five hundred pounds per annum, and diftributed amongft them. To render this part of his charity as beneficial as poffible, he would inquire of perfons the moft noted for integrity and liberality, who were the moft neceffitous and deferving poor in their refpective neighbourhoods. When he had been informed who they were, he went to their houfes, that he might judge farther, by meagre looks, number of children, mean furniture, and other circumftances, in what degree it might be fit to affift them. He always kept and produced exact and regular accounts of the money intrufted to him, but in time his fidelity became to be fo well known, that many of his contributors would not receive them. Sometimes the fums intrufted to him for the fervice of the poor were fo large, that he was enabled to commit a part of it to thofe, whom he knew to be charitably difpofed like himfelf;

ſelf; and when they had given it to ſuch as appeared to be neceſſitous, they would return to him an account of their names and caſes *.

In theſe diſtributions Mr. Firmin ſometimes conſidered others beſides the mere poor, particularly the poorer ſort of miniſters. He uſed to ſend, upon occaſion, no leſs than ten pounds to a clergyman in debt, if his difficulties aroſe from a ſmall income or a large family; taking care firſt of all to be aſſured that he was a man of probity and merit. He once aſked a friend concerning a clergyman, whoſe name is not recorded, what ſort of a man he was? his friend anſwered, "That his mind was much "above his purſe, for he was charitable, "ingenious, learned, and a father amongſt "young ſcholars who were promiſing "men; but his living not worth above "eighty or ninety pounds per annum." Mr. Firmin replied, "I have done much "for that man:" and his friend aſſured him that his liberality had never been better placed. Upon the death of this clergyman, his widow was aſked, whe-

* Life, page 43, 44.

ther there had not been ſome acquaintance, between her huſband and Mr Firmin. " She ſaid the acquaintance was
" not much, but the friendſhip great.
" Her huſband had been acquainted with
" many perſons of quality, and had expe-
" rienced their liberality through the
" whole courſe of his life, becauſe his
" addreſs as well as his merit was ſo re-
" markable. But of his many benefac-
" tors, Mr. Firmin had done moſt for
" him both in life and death. When
" her huſband died, his effects would not
" pay his debts, upon which ſhe was ad-
" viſed by a clergyman, to propoſe a
" compoſition with the creditors, that
" ſeeing every one could not be fully
" paid, yet all might receive a part. She
" conſulted Mr. Firmin upon this, who
" approved the advice, and was one of
" the firſt that ſubſcribed the compoſi-
" tion, but remitted to her his whole
" debt, and endeavoured to procure ſome-
" thing from others, in which he did not
" ſucceed according to his wiſh; but he
" himſelf made her a preſent of a good
" Norwich ſtuff, that very well clothed
" her, and her four children *."

* Life, Page 45 46.

Mr.

Mr. Firmin certainly judged very properly in thinking, that charity ſhould not be confined entirely to the very loweſt orders of poor. Such as have lived in reputation and credit, have more wants and finer feelings than thoſe who have been always habituated to poverty, and are deſerving of the peculiar attention of the benevolent, whom Providence hath ſupplied with the means of affording occaſional relief, in larger ſums than pence and ſhillings.

" I do not love (ſays the celebrated " Pope Ganganelli) in one of his enter- " taining letters (if they be his letters), " I do not love beſtowing drop by drop, " or tying one's ſelf down to regular " alms-giving, ſo as to have nothing left " for an object in extreme want. It is " better to reſcue one or two families " from diſtreſs, than to ſcatter a few " pieces at random without compleating " any purpoſe. Beſides, it would be pro- " per to have always a ſum in reſerve " for extraordinary caſes, for by this " œconomy you will have a remedy at " hand for unforeſeen contingencies. Do " not give into that wrong notion of

" charity which, without conſidering
" either birth or extraction, would have
" all its objects clothed and fed like
" the meaneſt of the people. Charity
" humbles nobody, and ſhould be pro-
" portioned to circumſtances and con-
" ditions *."

* Vol. I. Letter 50, to Count * * *.

C H A P.

CHAP. III.

Mr Firmin's Attention to Christ's Church and St. Thomas's Hospitals; to the Irish and French Refugees; and to other Public and Private Charities. Some Account of Bishop Compton.

MR. FIRMIN, during the last twenty-three or twenty-four years of his life, was one of the governors of that noble and useful charity Christ's Church Hospital, to which he was a great friend and benefactor. King Edward VI. that miracle of piety, learning, and discernment, the glory of our nation, and the admiration of all foreigners, was its original founder. He was moved to this benevolent action by a sermon, which Bishop Ridley * preached before him, just as he was about to leave this world; which circumstance did not lessen his concern for the happiness of those who were to remain in it.

* Ridley's Life of Bishop Ridley, page 396, 399.

Christ's

Chriſt's Church Hoſpital was allotted for orphans and ſuch as were naturally helpleſs; and it hath been greatly enlarged and improved, ſince the time when it was firſt erected, by the benefactions of ſeveral generous and humane perſons.

The children are educated in all parts of uſeful learning; and by this means ſuch as would otherwiſe be a burden and even a nuiſance to the public are qualified for rendering it the greateſt ſervices. The girls are about ſeventy in number, but above a thouſand boys are maintained, clothed, and inſtructed, in writing, drawing, mathematics, the learned languages, and any other branch of knowledge, as their various geniuſes may incline them, which is always attended to by the maſters, who are men of abilities, and frequently of great eminence in their ſeveral profeſſions.

Mr. Firmin procured many and very conſiderable donations for this hoſpital, and was unwearied in his endeavours to ſee the charity of the generous properly applied. The Honourable Sir Robert Clayton, deſiring to make proviſion for a mathematical maſter, thought fit to propoſe,

propoſe, and, and by his intereſt with ſome great perſons at court, was enabled to procure, the eſtabliſhment of a mathematical ſchool, for bringing up forty boys, well ſkilled in the Latin tongue, to a perfect knowledge of the art of navigation. Seven thouſand pounds had been given by a citizen of London for this purpoſe, but the fund, out of which it was paid reverted to the crown at the Reſtoration. King Charles II. however, was pleaſed to grant this money, that it might be applied to the purpoſes for which it was deſigned. Sir Robert, who had been the chief inſtrument in procuring it, was highly pleaſed with his ſucceſs; and he was reſolved to do ſomething likewiſe at his own expenſe. Gratitude to God who had raiſed him from a very dangerous fit of ſickneſs, in which his life was deſpaired of, led him to think of thus expreſſing his obligations. Mr. Firmin had the happineſs of being very inſtrumental towards his recovery, by perſonally attending him, and giving immediate notice to the phyſicians of ſeveral ſymptoms *.

* Life, page 57.

What

What Sir Robert determined upon was the building a ward for girls in this hoſpital, and he committed the management of the affair to Mr. Firmin, who ſet about it with great alacrity and diligence. At whoſe charge it was done, was then kept a ſecret; but when near four thouſand pounds had been laid out upon it, and it remained ſtill unfiniſhed, party diſputes ran high in the city, and thoſe, who would not declare for the court doctrine of paſſive obedience (amongſt whom were Sir Robert and his faithful friend and agent Mr. Firmin) were put out of all poſts of power and authority. Then it was that Mr. Firmin broke ſilence, and upbraided thoſe excluding governors, for depriving the hoſpital of ſo great a benefactor as the builder of that ward *. His arguments, however, were borne down by a great majority of the governing citizens, who, either through ſtupidity, or fear, or private intereſt, defended with great zeal that ſlaviſh and degrading opinion, ſo entirely repugnant to common ſenſe, and to the conſtitution of England.

* Life, page 58.

Mr. Firmin, besides being employed for Sir Robert, was also the agent for another gentleman, who chose to conceal his name, but expended above four hundred and thirty pounds in building a ward for the sick, that being kept apart they might not infect the healthy and sound, if the small pox, or any other contagious distemper, should happen to get in amongst the children, as is often the case. He also received from other persons two thousand, two hundred and forty one pounds, which he took care properly to dispose of and account for. At the charge also of one of his friends, he laid leaden pipes to convey the water to the several offices of the hospital, and and bought a large cistern, which, with the pipes, cost about two hundred pounds. These were great conveniences to the house, and especially to the orphans, who before fetched up the water which they used on their backs; which, as it was too laborious an employment for their tender years, so it likewise made some of the apartments and the clothes of the children dirty; things which ought carefully to be guarded against in all charitable institutions.

Besides

Besides this, he built a school at Hartford for the hospital children, where many of them are still boarded. The school cost five hundred and forty-four pounds, of which he received, by the charity of ten persons, four hundred and eighty-eight pounds: as to the balance of fifty-six pounds, it lay upon himself for any thing that appears to the contrary. It was also entirely at his own expense, that he set up a clock and dial for the use of the hospital, repaired all the walls, and built two brick-houses, to be disposed of to such officers, as the governors of the hospital should see fit *.

It was Mr. Firmin's custom to be present every Lord's Day at five in the evening with the orphans at their public devotions; for at that time prayers were read, and an anthem sung by select voices, in the chorus of which all joined. After this they sat down to supper at the several tables, under the care of their matrons. Here Mr. Firmin observed the behaviour, both of them, their officers and attendants, commending or admonishing as there was occasion. To

* Life, page 58. The above is testified by a certificate under the clerk's hand.

this

this ſight he invited, at different times all his friends, whether of the town or country; and before they went away he would lead them to the orphan's box, to which they contributed as they ſaw fit. A certain perſon who came from the country, was ſo well pleaſed, after having ſeen the order and method of the hoſpital, that, on returning home, he made his will, and gave very conſiderably to the place. Here it ſhould not be forgotten, that Mr. Firmin very carefully inſpected the management of the food provided for the uſe of the hoſpital. This is a matter too much neglected by governors of charities, and overſeers of the poor, as thouſands of our fellow creatures know to their ſorrow. He would not ſuffer any negligence of this ſort; and once when the children's ſuppers were prepared, thinking that one of the portions was too ſmall, he carried it immediately into the kitchen and weighed it himſelf. It proved, however, to be of full weight, and ſo the cook eſcaped the ſevere reproof, which any want of regularity or due care would have drawn from him *.

* Life, page 60, 61.

St. Thomas's Hoſpital in Southwark, was another of the pious King Edward's foundations, and intended for the relief of the lame, wounded, and ſick. On the care of this Mr. Firmin entered in the year 1693, when Sir Robert Clayton, being then Father of the city of London, was choſen preſident of the ſaid hoſpital, which office he thought fit to accept. On taking a view of it, he found that it was ſadly gone to ruin. The ground about the lodgings not having been cleared away for a long ſpace of time, was raiſed ſo high, that the patients lay as it were in a cellar, in a cloſe confined air, than which nothing could have been more injurious. The roof and the walls alſo were exceedingly out of repair, and it rained through even upon the beds. It was in vain to think of any thing elſe than rebuilding, nor could that be delayed without great injury and damage to the materials; for ſome part prevented the workmen's pulling it down, by falling of itſelf *.

Sir Robert, knowing the activity and addreſs of his friend Mr. Firmin in all

* Life, page 72.

works

works of charity, caused him to be chosen one of the governors. He found that the revenues of the hospital were insufficient, either for the purposes of rebuilding or repairing, unless the sick and wounded were denied relief; an expedient which he could not bear to think of, and therefore immediately set himself about procuring subscriptions. The president was pleased to give three hundred pounds, and the governors, several merchants, and other rich traders were very liberal, subscribing from twenty to an hundred pounds each. Without doubt the most of this money would have been contributed, though Mr. Firmin had not been the solicitor for it; yet it was computed by knowing and capable judges, that the subscriptions were greater by a thousand pounds than they would have been, had not he used his powerful interest. The charge being computed, and the money in part raised, materials were also to be provided, and workmen to be consulted and agreed with. Mr. Firmin was constant in attending the committee appointed for that purpose, and the master-builders made their most frequent applications to

him,

him, whilſt he was very careful to overſee their proceedings *.

One thing troubled the governors very much, which was, that they were obliged to rebuild the church of the pariſh, in which the hoſpital ſtood. The ſum neceſſary for this purpoſe, being ſome thouſands of pounds, could not be taken out of the revenue of the hoſpital, without great prejudice both to it and to the patients. It happened that the parliament was then about ſettling a tax for the finiſhing St. Paul's Cathedral; and the governors petitioned the houſe of commons, for ſome ſhare in that tax towards rebuilding St. Thomas's Church. But becauſe many other pariſhes prayed for the like aſſiſtance at the ſame time, the houſe upon a debate in a grand committee, reſolved that only St. Paul's and Weſtminſter Abbey ſhould have any ſuch proviſion allowed them. Mr. Firmin was much grieved at this reſolution, but being determined that no method ſhould be left untried, he and another of the governors ſet themſelves, that very night, to draw up ſeveral rea-

* Life, page 74.

ſons

ſons, ſhewing that St. Thomas's Church, had a claim to ſome favour in preference to the reſt. They uſed ſuch diligence as to get theſe reaſons publiſhed againſt the next morning, and he and his aſſociate gave copies of them to the members as they entered the houſe, telling them that they muſt not expect to have the ſick and wounded ſeamen cured, if they did not pay ſome attention to their requeſt.

The effect was, that the houſe took the matter again into conſideration, and allowed three thouſand pounds to the hoſpital for the uſe deſired. The obtaining this, cauſed Mr. Firmin to return home with more pleaſure and ſatiſfaction than if an eſtate of that value had fallen to himſelf *.

In the year 1680 and 1681, the French Proteſtants, driven from their own country by the cruel perſecutions of Lewis XIV. came in great numbers to England, and made new work for Mr. Firmin's charity and zeal. Of all objects he thought thoſe the moſt deſerving, who choſe rather to ſuffer than to ſecure

* Life, page 75, 76.

their

their eaſe by doing violence to the ſacred dictates of conſcience. Whether the opinions of the ſufferers agreed with his own or not, weighed but little with him; ſincerity in what they profeſſed was what he thought rendered them deſerving the help of every friend to virtue and religion *. Turks and Jews, ſhould they be driven from any country, purely on account of their faithful adherence to that religion, of the truth of which they were fully perſuaded, ought to be eſteemed and received as perſecuted for righteouſneſs' ſake.

The ſufferings of the French Proteſtants exceeded all that can be conceived or imagined. Biſhop Burnet, who was an eye witneſs to them, ſays, "That "the perſecution was ſo much beyond "all the common meaſures of barbarity "and cruelty, that I confeſs they ought "not to be believed, unleſs I could give "more poſitive proofs of them, than are "now proper to be brought forth, ſince "it might prove fatal to many who are "yet in the power of their enemies †." But of that which Biſhop Burnet was

* Life, page 51. † Travels, Letter V.

ſilent about, from a regard to the ſufferers, the world hath been informed ſince by means of a pamphlet written in French, where the method of dragooning the Proteſtants is briefly deſcribed *. They were plundered; they were tortured; they were murdered with every circumſtance of the moſt unrelenting cruelty; and at the ſame time every method was uſed to prevent their eſcaping out of the kingdom. However, no leſs than one hundred and fifty thouſand fled to other countries, and vaſt numbers of them came hither.

The firſt thing to be done, which was a matter of no ſmall difficulty, was to provide lodgings for the large multitude who reſorted to London, where the rent of houſes is exceedingly high. Mr. Firmin, whoſe active mind always quickly ſuggeſted the beſt expedients, propoſed to the lord mayor and court of aldermen that the peſt-houſe †, then quite empty

* There are ſome extracts from this piece, if I remember right, in a valuable tract intitled Popery always the Same.

† London being formerly more ſubject to contagious diſtempers than now, this building was deſigned for the infected in order that the plague might not ſpread univerſally.

of patients, ſhould be devoted to the ſervice of theſe ſtrangers: and ſeveral hundreds of them were accommodated in that large and convenient place. As for relief in money, many thouſands of pounds were raiſed for them, moſt of which went through Mr. Firmin's hands; and to contribute in the moſt effectual manner to their ſupport, he ſet up a linen manufacture at Ipſwich; which was the right way not only to prevent their being burdenſome, but even to render them of ſervice to the public at large. Towards the eſtabliſhment of this manufacture, erecting a place of worſhip, and purchaſing ſome neceſſaries, he himſelf contributed near one hundred and fifty pounds. Mr. Firmin's labours for the refugees were of a long continuance, for the perſecution was carried on in France for ſeveral years with violence and rigour. In 1693, there were ſuch numbers here, who needed relief, that beſides granting them a brief, King William allowed them out of his privy purſe, one thouſand pounds per month, for thirty-nine months ſucceſſively. The diſtribution of this royal bounty, was committed to the care of two biſhops,

two

twoknights, and a gentleman, but the management of it was left almoſt entirely to Mr. Firmin, ſometimes with, but more commonly without their inſpection *.

Whilſt Mr. Firmin had this important charge upon his hands, he was obliged to exert himſelf alſo in behalf of other objects, whoſe diſtreſſes called loudly upon the benevolent, whilſt the near relation in which they ſtood to this country, gave them a peculiar claim to the aſſiſtance of every inhabitant of it. Theſe were the Iriſh nobility, gentry, clergy, and others of all ranks and conditions, who fled into England from the cruel proſcriptions of James II. After the crown of theſe realms had been ſettled on King William and Queen Mary, King James ſtill retained a number of friends in Ireland, which abounded with Papiſts; and in March 1689 he landed there, with about five thouſand French ſoldiers and two hundred officers whom Louis XIV. had furniſhed him with †.

The Iriſh Papiſts, whenever it had been in their power, had always treated

* Life, page 51,—54.

† Tindal's Continuation of Rapin, vol. III. page 79, 80.

the Proteſtants with the moſt unrelenting cruelty. The bloody maſſacre in 1641 can never be forgotten. It has been computed that in the ſpace of a few months upwards of one hundred and fifty thouſand were actually murdered, and as many more forcibly driven from their habitations, and compelled to endure all the miſeries of cold, hunger, and nakedneſs *. Many then living had been eye witneſſes of the barbarities committed by the Papiſts, who, having now a king of their own religion at their head, and a French army to aſſiſt them, filled the Proteſtants, as may well be ſuppoſed, with horror and dread. King James ſufficiently evidenced the ſavageneſs of his own diſpoſition in ſeveral inſtances, and particularly in an act paſſed by his parliament, which attainted near three thouſand at once of both ſexes and of all ages. Amongſt theſe were two archbiſhops, one duke, ſeventeen earls, ſeven counteſſes, twenty-eight viſcounts, two viſcounteſſes, ſeven biſhops, eighteen barons, thirty-three baronets, fifty-one knights, eighty-three clergymen, two

* Rapin, vol. II. page 386, note ii.

thousand one hundred and eighty-one esquires and gentlemen; all of whom were declared traitors and adjudged to suffer the pains of forfeiture and death. A clause was also inserted, by means of which (besides what was enacted against these,) the estate of almost every Protestant in the kingdom was forfeited *. And that the Protestants might not be able to entertain a hope, that the rage and fury would cool down, the king gave up the royal prerogative of pardoning, after a certain time limited by the act; so that there was no way left of avoiding the terrible destruction but by a timely flight.

To England they came, which has long been the refuge of the persecuted and oppressed, and amongst their numerous friends Mr. Firmin was eminently distinguished by his activity and diligence. A brief was granted, of which he was one of the commissioners. Besides what might be raised by the brief, the ministers, church-wardens, and collectors of every parish in England, were to give an account of what sums they had severally

* Tindal's Continuation, vol. III. page 87, 88.

collected. Therefore on many post days for a long time together, several hundreds of letters came to his hands, and he himself received many collections, and paid them into the chamber of London. The money given by the king and queen was also intrusted to his management; and it was in a great measure owing to his solicitation that the royal bounty was obtained *.

The refugees were so numerous and their necessities so great, as to require a second brief; and the sum total, which went through Mr. Firmin's hands, was fifty-six thousand five hundred, sixty-six pounds, seven shillings and sixpence. The money was to be distributed by a particular number of commissioners, but he was the most constant of any man at their meetings, often attending from morning to night, without allowing himself any time for his meals. Besides the sums regularly distributed, he obtained and gave more considerable sums in a private way to particular persons, whose rank and quality seemed to render it im-

* Life, page 65.

proper

proper for them to take off the common ſtock, or whoſe neceſſities required more than could be allowed out of it. For it was incumbent upon the managers to give no cauſe of offence, or lay themſelves open to the charge of partiality, ſince any thing of that ſort might have checked the benevolence of the public *.

But affairs in Ireland ſoon took a happy turn. In the month of July 1689, King William gained an important victory on the banks of the river Boyne, and obliged King James again to take refuge in France, his adherents being forced to ſubmit to the conqueror. Their country being thus delivered, the Proteſtant refugees were enabled with ſafety to return to their houſes, employments, and eſtates; and Mr. Firmin ſtrenuouſly exerted himſelf to furniſh them with neceſſaries for their journey. By a ſpeedy removal they were materially benefited, and the charitable and generous of this nation, enabled to give larger aſſiſtance to ſuch others as ſtood in need of their kindneſs. Mr. Firmin obtained great ſums for this purpoſe; and one gentleman (Sir

* Life, page 66.

Thomas Cook) gave no leſs than fifteen hundred pounds, an inſtance of generoſity which deſerves to be recorded.

Mr. Firmin's kindneſs was ſenſibly felt and gratefully remembered, as appears by the following letter, from the moſt Reverend the Archbiſhop of Tuam and ſeven other biſhops.

TO MR. THOMAS FIRMIN.

SIR,

Being occaſionally met together at Dublin on a public account, and often diſcourſing of the great relief which the Proteſtants of this kingdom found amongſt their brethren in England in the time of our late miſeries, we cannot treat that ſubject without as frequent mention of your name, who ſo cheerfully and entirely devoted yourſelf to that miniſtry. We conſider with all thankfulneſs, how much the public charity was improved by your induſtry, and we are witneſſes of your indefatigable pains and faithfulneſs in the diſtribution, by which many thouſands are preſerved from periſhing. We know alſo, that ſome who refuſed to take out of the common ſtock, as being deſirous to cut off occaſion of

murmurs,

murmurs, were however, by your mediation, comfortably ſubſiſted by private benevolences. We doubt not, but you and they have the earneſt of your reward in the peace of your minds, which we pray God to fill with comforts and illuminate with his truths, making his grace to abound in them, who have abounded in their charity to others. And we intreat, that you, and all ſuch as you know to have had their parts in this ſervice, would believe, that we ſhall ever entertain a grateful remembrance of it; as ſome teſtimony whereof, we deſire you, for yourſelf in particular, to receive this acknowledgment of your kindneſs to our brethren, and therein to your much obliged

and moſt humble ſervants,

J. TUAM.

W. Clonfert. N. Waterford.
B. Fernleigh. R. Clogher.
S. Elpin. W. Raphoe.
E. Cork and Roſs.

This was a letter very worthy of the epiſcopal character, and a noble teſtimony of the high regard in which Mr. Firmin was held. Nor was this the only tribute of praiſe which he received on that

 occaſion,

occaſion, for a reverend dean, who had been one of the ſufferers, addreſſed a poem to him " on his incomparable " charity and generous induſtry in reliev- " ing the Iriſh refugees." In it he is compared, for his activity and zeal, to thoſe miniſtring ſpirits, who, warmed with the divineſt principle of love, are ever on the wing, and fly without ceaſing to every place where diſtreſs calls for their aid, or they may be able to adminiſter joy. Preachers moved their congregations, but the eloquence of his tongue, inſpired by the feelings of his heart firſt moved many of the preachers; and as the ſufferers had loſt all things, ſo he for a while ſeemed loſt to all things but them. Such are the leading ſentiments of the poem*, the whole of which is expreſſive of the higheſt admiration and the warmeſt gratitude, nor is there the leaſt need of any grains of allowance for the poetical licenſe. Mr. Firmin was always very diligent in buſineſs, but more abundantly ſo in acts of kindneſs

* The writer of Mr. Firmin's Life has given it entire, but the verſification is not ſufficiently ſmooth to pleaſe modern ears, on which account it is not inſerted here.

and

and charity; and he juſtly deſerved (if it be poſſible for a mortal to deſerve) *the title of a godlike man.*

At a large expenſe he apprenticed many boys, and contributed to ſet them up in trade, if they had ſerved diligently and faithfully. He juſtly conſidered this as a ſort of charity, that extended to the whole of a man's life, and might be the ground of many charities in future, as it ſupplied them with the means of riſing in the world, and of doing in time that for others, which ſome had done for them. The clergy of London and other dignified perſons of the church, often aſſiſted him very liberally in this good and uſeful work *. And there was one great clergyman, of whom he never ſpoke without particular reſpect and honour, on account of the vigour and active zeal, by which he was eminently diſtinguiſhed in all the offices of religion and humanity; this was the honourable Dr. Henry Compton, Biſhop of London †: whoſe zeal againſt Popery, when it was favored by the court; whoſe oppoſition to arbitrary power, when our liberties

* Life, page. 76. † ibid, p. 55.

were in real danger; whoſe unwearied endeavours to promote virtue and piety, and whoſe generoſity in relieving the diſtreſſed, have raiſed him to no ſmall degree of eminence amongſt the uſeful and worthy characters who have adorned this nation. Mr. Firmin was a witneſs to his conduct when in the ſtrength and vigour of life, and ſaw how nobly he acted in difficult and trying ſeaſons, boldly oppoſing the will of his prince, rather than acting contrary to the laws of his country; and ſtanding forth as a champion for the Proteſtant cauſe, when at leaſt to connive at Popery was eſſential to a man's intereſt at court *. The biſhop was alſo ſenſible of Mr. Firmin's worth, and had a very high opinion of him.

There were at that time particular collections made every winter in the churches about London, for the uſe of the

* He was ſuſpended, in the year 1686, from all epiſcopal and other eccleſiaſtical juriſdiction, for refuſing to comply with an illegal mandate of King James's in favour of popery. When the Prince of Orange landed, the Princeſs Anne put herſelf under his protection, and he headed a little army, who requeſted that he would be their commander. He bore alſo a diſtinguiſhing part in the glorious Revolution.

the poor in and near the city. Mr Firmin was the man who ſolicited the king's letter for making theſe collections, and took care of diſtributing his majeſty's and the biſhop of London's letters to the ſeveral miniſters of the churches in London to be by them read and publiſhed. He waited on the lords of the treaſury to receive the royal bounty, and when all the moneys were collected, and paid into the chamber of London to be divided amongſt the ſeveral pariſhes, by the lord mayor and the biſhop, no man could proportion their reſpective dividends with ſuch exactneſs as Mr. Firmin. This was well known to their lordſhips, who therefore ſeldom made any alterations in his diſtributions. In all theſe matters, the church-wardens made their application to and received their orders from him, for which purpoſe the biſhop would many times ſign blank papers, truſting that Mr. Firmin would not fail of properly diſcharging the truſt repoſed in him, and as to the lord mayor he was always ready to give his hand

The whole of this charity was for ſo many years under Mr. Firmin's management,

ment, that he, happening to die ſome days before chriſtmas, the king's letter was not obtained till the twelfth of January following; and when the collection was brought in from the ſeveral pariſhes, the managers were at a loſs how to diſtribute it, and were glad to take their directions from his pattern *.

Much more however remains to be ſaid of him, before we come to ſpeak of his diſſolution, for he was continually doing good, in methods as various, as the occaſions which offered themſelves to call forth his zeal and abilities into action.

* Life, p. 54.

CHAP. IV.

Mr. Firmin's undaunted Zeal in the Service of his Country as a Politician and a Patriot. His Enmity to all kinds of Licentiousness: his Endeavours to promote Virtue and Piety; his strong Abhorrence of the Crime of Swearing, and the Method which he used to check this Vice in any of his Acquaintance.

THOSE who have the least acquaintance with the English History, need not to be informed, that King James II. was excluded from the throne of these realms, for his open attempts to subvert our religion and liberties. The establishment of Popery and arbitrary power appeared to be his darling objects; and those, who opposed his attempts, had much to fear from his vindictive temper *. The unhappy persons

* See the preamble to the Declaration setting forth the reasons for exalting the Prince and Princess of Orange to the throne. *Rapin*, vol. II. p. 794—5.

who

who had joined themſelves to the Duke of Monmouth in his raſh enterprize, were treated with the moſt unrelenting cruelty, as were many others whom the king ſuſpected to be unfriendly to his views. Amongſt others Mr. Samuel Johnſon, a divine of the church of England, who was a man of great learning and a moſt exemplary character, felt the weight of his vengeance. He had ſuffered impriſonment for ſeveral years, not having been able to pay a fine, laid on him for writing in the cauſe of liberty. Inſtead of endeavouring to free himſelf from confinement by mean ſubmiſſions, he cauſed to be printed and diſperſed ſeveral ſmall pieces againſt Popery. This was very diſpleaſing to the king, but that which incenſed his majeſty to the higheſt degree was, "His "humble and hearty addreſs to all the "Proteſtants in the preſent army." In this he endeavoured to diſplay the reaſons, which ought to prevent them from being the inſtruments of the court in ſubverting our religion and government. His arguments made ſuch impreſſions on the minds of the officers and ſoldiers, that his addreſs &c. was thought very conducive

conducive to the Revolution, as most of the army went over to the Prince of Orange about two years afterwards. For the present, it was the cause of no small sufferings to Mr. Johnson. He was condemned to be degraded *ex officio et beneficio*, to stand three times in the pillory, to pay a fine of five hundred marks, and to be whipped from Newgate to Tyburn. The whipping, which was rigorously inflicted December 1, 1686, he bore with amazing firmness; and, notwithstanding what he had suffered, continued, though in prison, to employ his pen in the service of his country *.

It was, no doubt, imagined by the tyrant James, that punishments, so dreadfully severe, would cause universal terror; but there always have been some men of brave spirits even in the most dangerous times to stand up for our liberties; and to Mr. Firmin's honour be it spoken, he was one of that number. He was ever mindful of those who suffered for conscience' sake, or for asserting our just rights. He printed a great many sheets

* See his life in the Biographia Britannica, or the Biographical Dictionary, also Burnet's and Rapin's Histories.

and

and ſome books, the deſign of which was, to excite his countrymen to look about them, and prevent the ruin, which threatened our conſtitution and laws. Like a great and good citizen he ſtood firm, and, in very dangerous times, purſued thoſe meaſures, to which his duty as a member of ſociety directed him, not moved by the fear of thoſe conſequences, which, without doubt, intimidated many. More particularly he ſet himſelf to oppoſe with great vigour that attempt of the king's on our religion and liberties, which was rendered plauſible and inſnaring by an appearance of juſtice and moderation. This was his *Declaration for toleration and indulgence in religion*, which he commanded to be read in all the churches, merely on his own authority in contradiction to expreſs acts of parliament. Mr. Firmin uſed his utmoſt endeavours to convince the public of the very bad tendency and deſign of this ſpecious Declaration. He expended conſiderable ſums both in publiſhing and purchaſing ſuch pamphlets as were written with a view to open the eyes of the people, circulating and diſperſing them for the general good, at no ſmall coſt to himſelf.

himſelf *. Let it not however be imagined from hence, that he was an enemy to liberty of conſcience in its greateſt extent; never did any man poſſeſs a more liberal and enlarged mind. But he well knew that, if the king had a right to diſpenſe with the obſervance of one law, he might do the ſame with regard to all, and then a parliament would be uſeleſs, and our conſtitution totally ſubverted. This induced him ſtrenuouſly to oppoſe the diſpenſing power, and though he was very ſenſible that no worth or excellency of character would protect any man from the cruel revenge of James, yet his heart was ſo filled with love to his country, that fear could find no place in it.

The ſucceſs of the Prince of Orange's attempt to reſcue this nation from Popery and ſlavery was very doubtful; and, if it had failed, thoſe, who favoured it would have become bleeding ſacrifices to their patriotic zeal. The fate of thoſe who joined the Duke of Monmouth was then freſh in every one's memory. Mr Firmin however furthered the deſign of the

* Life, page 61.

Prince

Prince to the very utmoſt of his power; and, when he was ſeated on the throne of theſe realms, our diſintereſted patriot had farther opportunities of teſtifying how true a friend he was to the national intereſt. A new government being happily eſtabliſhed, he contributed not a little towards its welfare and ſtability.

There has long been a prevailing inclination in this country to encourage French faſhions, which have a natural tendency to effeminate, and French manufactures, which muſt certainly impoveriſh us. This fondneſs for the productions of that vain fantaſtic people has been no ſmall ſource of their power and riches, which it behoves all true Britons to ſtrive to reduce within narrow bounds. In Mr. Firmin's days particularly it was a moſt important duty, when that ambitious Prince Louis XIV. aſpired to univerſal empire, and looked with an envious eye on Britain, which, after its happy deliverance by the Revolution, became the greateſt obſtacle to the accompliſhment of his proud deſigns.

To ruin and deſtroy us was the wiſh and deſire of Louis; and therefore Mr. Firmin moſt diligently promoted the manufactures

nufactures of the *Royal Lustring Company*, which was not only beneficial to the nation, by supporting numbers amongst our own poor, but also a vast prejudice to our grand enemy, by diminishing a considerable source of their riches. He, together with Mr. Renew (who was one of the French refugees) were at much expense, to prevent the bringing over silks from France, and those other commodities, which several merchants, encouraged by the vain and frivolous who were more fond of the trifling ornaments of dress, than solicitous about the welfare of their country, ventured, in spite of the laws, to import. Mr. Renew's conduct was highly approved of by parliament, who voted him an honourable reward for his services *; and Mr. Firmin likewise deserved well of the public; for both these gentlemen exposed themselves to great danger. They ran the hazard of their lives from the revenge of those whom they prosecuted, who were enraged beyond measure at the interruption of so gainful a trade, and the heavy losses to which a detection exposed them.

* Tindal's Continuation of Rapin, vol. III. p. 371—3.

It was Mr. Firmin who had the greateſt hand, and uſed the moſt effectual endeavours in procuring acts of parliament and rules of court for the ſupport and encouragement of that company, which was ſet up to furniſh us with ſilks manufactured amongſt ourſelves, which hath been a great advantage and credit to the nation. And they were his and Mr. Renew's agents, who gave either the firſt, or at leaſt very early intelligence of the French invaſion, which was deſigned to have followed the projected aſſaſſination of King William *. Both of theſe ſchemes were defeated by a timely diſcovery; and Mr. Firmin was an honoured inſtrument in ſaving us from the dreadful and impending miſchief.

But zealous as he was for the new government, and unwearied in his endeavours to promote its intereſts, yet he had a tender regard for thoſe clergymen, who, from motives of pure conſcience, ſcrupled taking the oaths of allegiance to it, and thereby loſt their preferments. The doctrines of paſſive obedience and on-reſiſtance, how abſurd ſoever they

* Life, page 63.

may

now appear, had been espoused and ıded by almost the whole body of the clergy, during the reign of Charles II. When James was on the throne, the same principles were inculcated; but his bold attempts to subvert our most sacred rights, caused a general alarm: and notwithstanding the clergy had been so long inculcating on the people, that kings were accountable only to God, great numbers of them were now convinced of their error, and allowed that resistance, in some cases, was lawful.

There were others, who, being too proud to acknowledge they had been mistaken, took the oaths required, but with secret reservations, and the help of those quibbling evasive methods, which too often serve to lull men's consciences asleep, when they sacrifice their integrity at the shrine of profit and ambition? some still remained, men of learning, virtue and piety, who resolving to adhere to what they had preached, refused to take the oaths; and government was laid under the unhappy necessity of depriving several as worthy of the places which they filled in the church as any of their contemporaries.

Mr.

Mr. Firmin felt himſelf ſtrongly diſpoſed to relieve them, and his charity, which was unconfined and impartial, began to exert itſelf in collecting money for theſe deprived Nonjurors, following a ſcheme drawn up by Mr. Kettlewell, a perſon of eminent piety, who himſelf was one of them.

Mr Firmin, however, did not proceed as he intended in purſuing this benevolent deſign, being deterred from it by ſome friends of high rank, who told him that this ſcheme was illegal, being calculated for the ſupport of the enemies of government *. Many perhaps will be of opinion that there could be nothing illegal in this humane action; for the Nonjurors were men of honour and conſcience, as appeared by the proof which they gave of their integrity, in adhering to the doctrines they had taught, though attended with the loſs of their valuable preferments. But Mr. Firmin, no doubt, thought that there was much force and ſtrength in the reaſons which his noble friends alledged againſt his ſcheme; and

* Dr. Birch's Life of Dr. Tillotſon, p.320.

indeed,

indeed, conſidering what various methods were uſed, again to bring in our former oppreſſor, very extraordinary caution was abſolutely neceſſary.

Mr. Firmin however, though a bold aſſertor of the liberties of the nation, was at the ſame time a determined enemy to all licentiouſneſs. Soon after the Revolution, it was thought adviſeable by the friends of that cauſe, to put a ſtop as far as was poſſible to all open profaneneſs; for which purpoſe many good laws were enacted, and ſeveral formed themſelves into a *Society for the Reformation of Manners*. To countenance the members of this excellent inſtitution, Mr. Firmin contributed by his advice, aſſiſtance and ſolicitations, as much as his leiſure from his other benevolent and uſeful undertakings would permit him: as for his purſe, that was always with them *. Theſe ſocieties were not confined to the capital, but were formed alſo in different parts of the country, and very good effects aroſe from them. Practical treatiſes were diſtributed, and ſuch an attention to the

* Life, page 63.

duties

duties of religion excited in numbers, as had not been known for a long time before *.

Mr. Firmin greatly approved the cuſtom of diſtributing plain, uſeful books, as they might not only prove beneficial to thoſe who ſhould then read them, but, being preſerved in a family, or diſperſed abroad, might become the means of doing good even to ſucceeding generations. The ſeeds of virtue and religion, when once ſown in a family, may continue for ages to bring forth ſome fruit, and the forming one mind to real piety may, in the iſſue of things, be attended with the happieſt conſequences to numbers. He often printed ten thouſand copies of the Scripture Catechiſm, of which his friend Dr. Worthington was ſuppoſed to be the author. Theſe were given to his ſpinners and their children, and to the children of Chriſt's church Hoſpital, whom he alſo engaged by rewards to learn it by heart, furniſhing them firſt with the means of inſtruction, and then propoſing further encouragement to ſuch as were diſpoſed to make a proper uſe

* Tindal's continuation of Rapin, vol. III. p. 374.

of them. Befides doing this, he lodged great numbers with bookfellers, to be fold at a cheaper rate than they could have afforded them, hoping that by this means they would be difperfed all over England. He valued this catechifm, because it was wholly in the words of Scripture, favoured no particular party or perfuafion, and was therefore calculated to be of general ufe as it did not lead the young into controverfies and debates *.

The members of the above-mentioned excellent focieties were men of worth and reputation, and they found greater benefit arifing from their ufeful and difinterefted labours, than merely exciting an attention to the external duties of religion. Swearing, drunkennefs, lewdnefs, and the profanation of the Lord's day, were alfo much reftrained; for they made it a rule to inform againft fuch as offended in thefe inftances; and threw that part of the fine which the law gave to them into a common ftock, for promoting their other charitable defigns.

As to fwearing, Mr. Firmin's zeal againft that moft inexcufable vice, which

* Life, page 50.

brings the moſt ſolemn oaths, once regarded as the bonds of ſociety, into contempt, was particularly warm. If in coffee-houſes, or other places, he heard any ſwearing, he would immediately challenge the forfeiture appointed by law, and he always applied it to the uſe of the poor; ſo that in the companies which he frequented, an oath was ſeldom heard. It was alſo his rule to raiſe the forfeiture according to the quality of the perſon offending; nor would he let a nobleman, or one of diſtinguiſhed rank, particularly a clergyman, get off at the ordinary rate. It was doubled or trebled upon them, eſpecially if ſuch were very common ſwearers, or their oaths more than ordinarily profane and impious. If any refuſed to pay what he demanded, he would tell them it was for the ſervice of the poor, whoſe collector and ſteward he was. If they ſtill refuſed, he aſſured them they ſhould be ſet down by him in the liſt of his incorrigible ſwearers, and that afterwards he never would own them for his acquaintance, or ſpeak to them as ſuch. And ſo highly was his friendſhip valued, that many noble perſons would not endure this laſt, but ſubmitted to do as he required.

required *. As to Mr. Firmin himſelf, the friend who firſt wrote his life declares "that though he converſed with him "daily for almoſt forty-four years, he never "once heard an oath from him." In this he was the more deſerving of commendation, becauſe his temper was naturally quick and warm, and he had oftentimes great provocations to anger, one of the principal cauſes of raſh and intemperate ſwearing. Would men of character and worth imitate his example, and alſo check the inexcuſable profaneneſs (and profaneneſs is ever inexcuſable) of any who in their company are guilty of it, it might be, and in various inſtances has been, attended with very good effects; for the extreme abſurdity of profane ſwearing ſeems to be univerſally acknowledged.

Such were Mr. Firmin's regards to the liberties of his country, and to the intereſts of virtue. What rendered him ſo fixed, ſteady, and uniform, was his firm perſuaſion of the truth and importance of the religion of Jeſus. He was a ſincere chriſtian from inquiry and conviction; and he ſought for the articles of his faith,

* Life, page 64.

as well as for rules for the conduct of his life in the pure word of God. His religious ſentiments were the reſult of cool, impartial examination; and as his attachment to theſe ſentiments, together with his zealous, but rational endeavours to promote an attention to them, has ever been reckoned a diſtinguiſhing part of his character, and cauſed him to be much taken notice of in his own days; the next chapter ſhall give an account of ſome of the moſt ſtriking particulars.

An Account of Mr. Firmin's religious Sentiments, and of his pious Endeavours to promote what appeared to him to be the true Doctrines of the Gospel. His great Kindness to Mr. Biddle, together with some Memoirs of that extraordinary Man. The Friendship of Archbishop Tillotson and Bishop Fowler for Mr. Firmin, with some Particulars concerning these eminent and worthy Divines. Other Instances of Mr. Firmin's Charity to the Sufferers for Religion.

IT may be reasonably supposed that Mr. Firmin's mind was impressed with sentiments of piety from his childhood. The Reader will naturally conclude that this was the case, from the character given of his parents in the first chapter; for such as are truly religious will endeavour, by all rational methods, to form the minds of others, particularly the minds of their children, to the same temper. The diligence and fidelity which

Mr. Firmin diſplayed when an apprentice afford alſo very good evidence of the pious care of his parents; and he gave other proofs, even in his youthful days, of an uncommon regard to the cauſe of religion. His mind was open to the reception of its pure and true doctrines, for he juſtly thought that ſincere attempts to underſtand the Scriptures, would always increaſe a man's love and regard for them.

His maſter was an Arminian, a hearer of the celebrated Mr. John Goodwin, who preached in Coleman Street *. His warm zeal for liberty led him to be a ſtrenuous defender of thoſe by whom King Charles was brought to the block; for writing in defence of whom, he was excepted out of the act of grace which was paſſed at the Reſtoration †. He had alſo the hardineſs to introduce Arminianiſm amongſt the diſciples of Calvin, which, conſidering the zeal then diſplayed in behalf of that reformer's ſentiments

* Life, page 6.

† I do not remember that he ſuffered any puniſhment, but on Bartholomew day he was ejected from his living for Nonconformity. *Nonconformiſt's Memorial*, vol. I. page 151.

amongſt

amongſt his numerous partizans, was a very bold undertaking. But both his courage and his abilities were very great, and by hearing his learned diſcourſes, Mr. Firmin, who was naturally inquiſitive, became a free inquirer in matters of religion. In conſequence of this, he ſoon exchanged the harſh opinions of Calvin, in which he had been educated, for thoſe of Arminius and the remonſtrants, which, he thought, were not only more agreeable to reaſon, but alſo more honourable to God.

But the predeſtinarian notions were not the only ones which Mr. Firmin, after proper examination, rejected. His departure was much wider from that which is commonly ſtyled the orthodox faith. He was entirely ignorant of the learned languages, and alſo of the ſchool logic and philoſophy; but his underſtanding and judgment were very remarkable. And to theſe endowments of nature, improved by as much reading and converſation as his buſineſs allowed him time for, was united a ſincere love of truth, which rendered him much fitter to judge what were really the doctrines of revelation than moſt of thoſe who ſpend their whole lives in a college. Such have oftentimes a large ſtock of learning without any penetration, their knowledge conſiſting moſtly in an acquaintance with words, or the opinions of antiquated authors upon different ſubjects. And when learning and penetration have been united, there has been too much reaſon to complain, that, either through the prejudices of education, or the ſtrong biaſs of worldly intereſt, they have been generally employed in ſupporting what is commonly received, or hath had the ſanction of the public authority.

Mr. Firmin's mind was not thus ſhackled. Uninfluenced by thoſe prejudices which biaſs too many, he heard with attention what Mr. Goodwin advanced on man's free agency, and becoming at the ſame time acquainted with Mr. Biddle, was perſuaded, by his arguments, to adopt other notions likewiſe with regard to the nature of the Deity. He it was who convinced him, that the unity of God is a unity of perſon as well as of nature, and that there is no being whatſoever who can be likened unto the Moſt High *.

* Life, page 10.

That

That there are three Perſons in the Godhead equal in power and glory, is ſtill the doctrine generally received amongſt chriſtians; and at the time when Mr. Firmin began his religious inquiries the contrary had been advanced by very few in England.

A woman, who appeared to be a weak enthuſiaſt, was burnt for her heterodox notions on the ſubject of the Trinity in the reign of King Edward VI. much againſt the will of that mild and benevolent young prince, who ſubmitted entirely to the judgment of ſome of his learned inſtructors, when he ſigned the warrant. George Van-Parre likewiſe, a Dutchman, who led a moſt devout and exemplary life, ſuffered at the ſame time, and in the ſame manner for affirming "that the Father only was God *." Bartholomew Legate, and Edward Wightman, were alſo burnt in the reign of James I. That monarch, who was not a little vain of his theological abilities, and very fond of diſplaying them, admitted the former to his preſence, and endeavoured to convince him, that he

* Burnet's Hiſtory of the Reformation abridged, vol. II. page 81—82.

was in an error, but without effect. Neither the arguments, nor (what is more calculated to weigh with most minds) the hope of favour from his prince, could move him from his allegiance to the God and Father of all. The converts to these martyrs (if they made any) kept their opinions pretty much to themselves, very probably thinking, that it would be in vain to offer any defence of them to the public, at a time when men's prejudices were so strong, and the government so cruel and intolerant.

These circumstances were very discouraging to a young man, nor had the treatment, which his instructor met with any tendency to recommend his sentiments. But as soon as ever Mr. Firmin was fully convinced, that the peerless and unrivalled Majesty of God could be supported on no other principles than those which maintain his perfect unity, he set himself industriously to propagate this belief. Those were encouraged by him, whose abilities enabled them to defend the Unitarian doctrines in their writings, and at great pains and expense he dispersed these writings abroad. This

zeal

zeal exposed him both to reproach and danger, but such evils he always slighted, when they stood in competition with what he thought his duty. Mr. Biddle was a man of great note, much distinguished for real worth and excellency of character, and not a little by his many sufferings. He was likewise so highly valued, and so generously assisted by Mr. Firmin, whose attachment to him made his own character the more remarkable, that it would be a great omission not to say a few things concerning him; nor can an acquaintance with some circumstances, relating to this extraordinary person, fail of being agreeable to the Reader, if he sincerely love the patient, faithful friends of virtue and religion.

Mr. Biddle was born in the year 1615, at Wotton under Edge, in Gloucestershire, and had his education at the free-school near that place. His abilities were very promising, and even in his younger days, a singular piety of mind was observed in him *. When sent to

* Life of John Biddle, M. A. published in a collection of Unitarian Tracts, in 4to, printed in 1691, page 4. His Life has also a place in every Biographical work of any note.

Oxford,

Oxford, he prosecuted his studies with great assiduity, and was always more determined by reasons than by authority. In 1641, he took his degree of Master of Arts with much applause, and having received ample recommendations from the principal persons in that university, was chosen to be master of a free school in the city of Gloucester. In this situation he was highly esteemed for his diligence and abilities as a tutor, and also for his virtuous manners. He now set himself to read the Holy Scriptures with great attention; but no Socinian books whatever. Whilst he was perusing the sacred writings he fervently implored divine illumination, praying that the spirit of truth would lead him into all truth.

It cannot be supposed that a being, infinite in goodness and mercy, would suffer such a man to fall into any dangerous error. Nor can it on the other hand be imagined, that God enlightens the mind so far as to enable it to judge rightly on every point of controversy. The most learned, sober, and devout men have differed widely in their sentiments; from whence we may infer that this

diversity

diverſity is, for ſome very wiſe reaſons, permitted. Mr. Biddle appears to have purſued his ſtudies, in the manner which became a lover of the Goſpel. It ſoon, however, appeared evident to him, that the common doctrine of the Trinity was not well grounded either in reaſon or revelation; being free and impartial in judging, he was alſo very open and generous in ſpeaking, and did, as occaſion offered, mention thoſe reaſons which induced him to queſtion it.

This cauſed an accuſation of hereſy to be brought againſt him, and, being ſummoned before the magiſtrates, he exhibited in writing a confeſſion of Faith, reſpecting the doctrine about which he was accuſed. This confeſſion not being thought ſatisfactory, he made another more explicit than the former. He was not ſuch an enthuſiaſt as to expoſe himſelf unneceſſarily to ſufferings, but endeavoured both to avoid impriſonment, and to keep a good conſcience. Yet this oppoſition did not intimidate, but led him to examine the Scriptures on this point with greater accuracy, by which means he was the more confirmed in his opinions. He then drew up what was

afterwards

afterwards publiſhed under the title of "Twelve arguments drawn out of the "Scriptures wherein the commonly re-"ceived opinion, touching the Deity of "the Holy Spirit, is clearly and fully "refuted." Theſe he communicated in manuſcript to ſome of his acquaintance, one of whom was ungenerous enough to betray him to the magiſtrates of Glouceſter, and to the committee of parliament then reſiding there. In conſequence of this, he was committed December 2d, 1645, to the common jail; which treatment was the more ſevere, as he was at that time ill of a dangerous fever. He did however procure a ſpeedy enlargement, through the intereſt of an eminent perſon in Glouceſterſhire, who gave ſecurity for his appearance whenever it ſhould pleaſe the parliament to ſend for him.

Six months after he had been ſet at liberty, he was ſummoned to appear at Weſtminſter, and he freely confeſſed to the committee papointed to examine him, "That he was ready to hear whatever "could be oppoſed to him, and if he "could not make out his opinions to be "true, he would then honeſtly confeſs his "error.

" error. What ſhall befal me (ſays he) " I refer to the diſpoſal of the all-wiſe " God, whoſe glory is dearer to me not " only than my liberty, but than my " life." He was here wearied out with tedious and expenſive delays, till at length his caſe being referred to the aſſembly of divines then ſitting at Weſtminſter; he often appeared before ſome of them, and gave them in writing, his Twelve Arguments againſt the Deity of the Holy Spirit, which were printed the ſame year. This made a great noiſe, the author was ſummoned to appear at the bar of the houſe of commons, and on being aſked Whether he owned the book and the arguments contained in it, he anſwered in the affirmative. Upon this he was remanded back to priſon, and the houſe ordered that his book ſhould be called in, and burnt by the hangman, which was accordingly done.

It has been ſaid, that in May 1648, the aſſembly of divines endeavoured to prevail on the parliament to put Mr. Biddle to death; certain it is, to their eternal ſhame and diſhonour, that they did actually procure a cruel, unjuſt, and perſecuting ordinance to be paſſed, making it *death* to oppoſe the ſentiments, which they ſaw fit to eſtabliſh, relating to the Deity of Chriſt and the Holy Spirit. It is hard to ſay, whether, in this affair, the aſſembly were moſt deſtitute of the temper which ought to adorn the miniſters of the Goſpel, or the parliament of that wiſdom which is neceſſary for lawgivers. The former were met as the repreſentatives of a very reſpectable part of the church to conſult about its intereſts; and the latter, the parliament, had ſolemnly engaged to reform religion both in diſcipline and doctrine. This then was a time when full liberty ſhould have been given to all to offer their ſentiments on religious matters; and Mr. Biddle's piety, modeſty and learning entitled him, at leaſt, to a fair and patient hearing. But ſo far was he from being able to obtain ſuch juſtice, that he probably owed his life merely to the great diſſenſions which aroſe amongſt the parliament on various ſubjects. Nevertheleſs, though he did not ſuffer death, his confinement was made cloſe for a while, until by means of the confuſed ſtate of public affairs, a ſort of univerſal toleration was introduced. He was then allowed more liberty by his keeper, who ſuffered him,

upon

upon security given, to go into Staffordshire, where a justice of the peace entertained him most courteously, and left him a legacy at his decease; which kindness was very seasonable, as he had been, whilst under restraint, at vast charges. The liberty which he enjoyed was, however, but of short continuance. Serjeant Bradshaw, president of the council of state, being informed of the indulgence which had been granted to him, caused him to be recalled and more strictly confined. It was unfortunate for Mr. Biddle that the charge of heresy and blasphemy rendered him so odious, that hardly any one would converse with him. Dr. Peter Gunning, afterwards Bishop of Ely, was the only divine who vouchsafed to visit this good man in his six years confinement and restraint. It ought likewise to be mentioned to the honour of the great and good Archbishop Usher, that passing through Gloucester at the time when Mr. Biddle's troubles began, he endeavoured to convince him that he was in an error, though without effect. Thus persecuted and forsaken, his whole substance was spent, and not having enough to pay for an ordinary meal, he was glad

to

to ſupport himſelf in the cheapeſt manner poſſible. A draught of milk, morning and evening, was very frequently all the ſuſtenance which he had. In theſe deplorable circumſtances, his learning and abilities did however at length procure him ſome comfortable relief, he being employed by Roger Daniel, of London, to correct an edition of the Greek Septuagint Bible, which was then about to be printed.

In 1651, the parliament publiſhed a general act of oblivion, and Mr. Biddle improved that liberty to which he was reſtored, by meeting with his friends every Lord's day for the purpoſe of expounding the Scriptures, and diſcourſing on them, being always ready to defend his own peculiar ſentiments whenever called upon. This made the London miniſters very uneaſy; but they could not prevent it. Dr. Gunning who had viſited him in his confinement, took the moſt rational method of ſtopping the progreſs of his opinions, by diſputing publicly with him in his meeting. Mr. Biddle acquitted himſelf ſo well on this occaſion, that he gained much credit both to himſelf and his cauſe, which ſome gentlemen

gentlemen of the oppofite party had the ingenuity to acknowledge, as they could not help admiring his learning and judgment, joined to a furprifing readinefs and fkill in the Holy Scriptures.

This happened in the year 1654, when he alfo publifhed a Scripture Catechifm, which brought him into frefh troubles. A complaint was made againft it in the houfe of commons; he was brought to the bar, and afked Whether he had written that book. He did not fee fit to avow it, as he had done, when he firft ftood before the fame tribunal, but anfwered, in the true fpirit of an Englifhman, by afking, "Whether it feemed reafonable "that one brought before a judgment "feat as a criminal fhould accufe himfelf?" To require this is without doubt againft all law and reafon, but herefy was accounted fo dreadful a crime, that, though it could not be clearly proved againft him (fince he refufed to betray his juft rights by making a confeffion of it), yet the catechifm was ordered to be burnt by the common hangman; and he, as the fuppofed author, was committed clofe prifoner to the Gate-houfe, and denied the ufe of pen, ink, paper, or the accefs

of

of any viſitant. And as if this were nothing, a bill was ordered to be brought into the houſe of commons for puniſhing him farther. But, ſince what had been already done was illegal, he obtained his liberty after ſix months impriſonment:

About a year after this, he was brought into greater danger. One Griffin, provoked to find that many of his congregation had embraced Mr. Biddle's notions concerning the Trinity, challenged him publicly to diſpute the matter. This Mr. Biddle would willingly have declined doing, not being forward to excite freſh clamours, unleſs ſome valuable ends were likely to be anſwered. Griffin, however, being importunate, the meeting was fixed, and a numerous audience being aſſembled, he aſked "If any man there "would deny that Chriſt was God moſt "high." Mr. Biddle reſolutely anſwered "I do deny it." The views of Griffin and his party were now anſwered. This zealot was by no means a match for Mr. Biddle in the way of argument, of which being conſcious, inſtead of giving him another meeting, as was propoſed, he accuſed him of blaſphemy, of which his denial of Griffin's queſtion was clear and poſitive proof, according to the ordinance againſt blaſphemy and hereſy then but lately made.

Oliver Cromwell, who had at that time the ſupreme command, under the title of Protector, was not willing, for certain political reaſons, that Mr. Biddle ſhould be brought to a trial, and therefore kept him a while in priſon, but at length baniſhed him to the iſle of Scilly, being weary of receiving petitions for and againſt him. Towards his ſupport in this confinement he allowed him one hundred crowns a-year. It is ſaid that this penſion was obtained by Mr. Firmin's ſolicitations, who was then indeed very young, but poſſibly by his agreeable addreſs and great courage he might recommend himſelf to the Protector's favour; for Mr. Firmin when an apprentice ventured to deliver a petition into the Protector's hand, praying that Mr. Biddle might be releaſed out of Newgate. Cromwell, though a friend to toleration, thought it his intereſt to appear zealous for religion, in the common acceptation of the word zeal, and thus replied to his young petitioner; "You curl-pate boy "you, do you think I will ſhew any fa- "vour

" vour to a man that denies his Saviour " and disturbs the government?" So strong was Mr. Firmin's attachment to Mr. Biddle, that he had lodged and boarded him gratis, thinking himself amply repaid by his improving conversation. In the year 1658, after about three years exile, the Protector, moved by the repeated intercessions of many of Mr. Biddle's friends, ordered him to be brought back to London; and nothing being then laid to his charge, he was set at liberty. Whilst in Scilly he had employed himself in studying the Scriptures; and being delivered from confinement, he again resumed his religious exercises, and his friends formed themselves into a church of which he was pastor.

On the death of Cromwell, a parliament was called, which, it was thought, would be dangerous to Mr. Biddle. He, therefore, took the advice of a noble friend, and retired into the country till the danger was over; when he returned to his pastoral care. On the restoration of Charles II. when the meetings of all dissenters were regarded as seditious,

* Birch's Life of Archbishop Tillotson, page 319.

Mr. Biddle held his in a private manner till June 1662, when himſelf and ſome of his friends being met for divine worſhip, they were all ſeized and ſent to priſon, without being admitted to bail. Upon their trial at the following ſeſſions, the hearers were fined twenty pounds each, and Mr. Biddle one hundred, and ordered to lie in priſon till that ſum was paid. In leſs than five weeks after, through the noiſomeneſs of the place and the want of air, he contracted a diſeaſe which put an end to his life on the 22d of September, 1662, in the forty-ſeventh year of his age. Thus was he numbered amongſt thoſe *who were ſlain for the word of God, and for the teſtimony of Jeſus*. He appears by the moſt authentic memorials to have cloſely ſtudied the Sacred Writings, eſpecially the New Teſtament, which he retained in his memory verbatim, not only in Engliſh, but in Greek, as far as the fourth chapter of the book of Revelations. In his moral conduct, he was not only irreproachable, but exemplary; he could not bear to hear a ſentence of Holy Writ uſed vainly or lightly, and his mind appeared at all times to be filled with the moſt awful reverence for the Deity.

Deity. When engaged in private devotion, he uſed frequently to proſtrate himſelf on the ground, after the manner of our Saviour in his agony; which poſture he uſed to recommend to his moſt intimate friends as the proper expreſſion of the deepeſt humiliation.

Mr. Firmin's love and regard for him were no ſmall proof of his worth; and it is highly probable, that the early acquaintance which he made with this moſt excellent man, contributed as much as any thing to his firm eſtabliſhment in virtuous and religious principles. It would have afforded good Mr. Biddle very little ſatisfaction had he made Mr. Firmin a convert to his opinions only: "He valued not his doctrines for ſpeculation "but practice, inſomuch that he would "not diſcourſe of thoſe points wherein "he differed from others, with thoſe that "appeared not religious according to their "knowledge. Neither could he bear "thoſe that diſſembled in profeſſion for "worldly intereſt *." He had the ſublime pleaſure of ſeeing Mr. Firmin improve under his inſtructions in the moſt valuable qualities, though he was re-

* Life prefixed to his Tracts.

moved to a better world, before he had an opportunity of ſeeing how very extenſively uſeful his young diſciple would be in this.

Mr. Firmin was at all times very free and open in declaring his Unitarian ſentiments, though they were then ſo obnoxious; but it was not till after the Revolution, that he greatly exerted himſelf in propagating them. Antecedent to that period, the friends of the conſtitution were ſo anxious about the national liberties, and ſuch as attended to religious inquiries ſo much taken up with the Popiſh controverſy, that but few had inclination or leiſure to attend to other diſputes. Theſe, and not any fear of danger, ſeem to be the principal reaſons, which induced Mr. Firmin in ſome degree to ſuppreſs his zeal during the earlier part of his life. The toleration act was no ſecurity to ſuch as avowed or publiſhed his ſentiments; on the contrary a very ſevere ſtatute was enacted by parliament againſt all who in any manner whatſoever oppoſed or denied the commonly received doctrines concerning the Trinity. Notwithſtanding this, Mr. Firmin was at great expenſe to have books printed explaining and defending the Unitarian notions, and theſe he freely gave away to as many as would read them. He revered the conſtitution, and made a point of obeying all the laws of his country, as far as they were of a civil nature. It appears, however, from many parts of his conduct, to have been his opinion, that magiſtrates had no right to prevent any man from profeſſing thoſe opinions, which his conſcience led him to adopt; nor would he ſubmit to that act of the legiſlature, which interfered with the peculiar province of the Almighty. But ſevere as the act was againſt all who oppoſed the common doctrines, Mr. Firmin was never put to any trouble, though his zeal againſt them was ſo well known. Nor did his reverend and right reverend friends decline acquaintance with him, thinking it their duty to give all the countenance in their power to ſo uſeful and good a man.

The illuſtrious Queen Mary, that ornament to her ſex, whoſe virtues added luſtre to a crown, condeſcended alſo to manifeſt the ſincereſt friendſhip towards him. She had heard with pleaſure and

approbation

approbation of Mr. Firmin's activity and diligence in promoting every charitable design. Being informed also that he was heterodox in the articles of our blessed Saviour's divinity, and the doctrine of satisfaction, she spoke to Archbishop Tillotson, and earnestly recommended it to him, to set his friend Mr. Firmin right in those points, which she deemed a matter of great moment and importance. The Archbishop replied that he had often attempted it, but in vain, not being able by any arguments he could use to alter the opinions which he had so long formed on these subjects. However, his Grace published the sermons which he had formerly preached against the Socinians, and sent Mr. Firmin one of the first copies from the press. He was not convinced either by Dr. Tillotson's reasonings, or his arguments from the Holy Scriptures; he caused a respectful answer to be drawn up and published, and himself gave the Archbishop a copy of it. To this his Grace, after he had read it, only said "my Lord of Sarum (meaning that very celebrated and worthy divine Bishop Burnet) shall humble your writers." Dr. Tillotson indeed in his behaviour to Mr. Firmin, as well as in a variety of other inſtances, gave full proof that a man may be poſſeſſed of the moſt ſhining abilities, and be raiſed to the higheſt ſtation, and yet retain all that humility and meekneſs of ſpirit, which is more amiable than common, in perſons ſo highly diſtinguiſhed as he was. He never expreſſed the leaſt degree of coldneſs towards Mr. Firmin on account of the anſwer made to his Sermons, but uſed to inquire in the ſame familiar manner as before "How does my ſon Giles," for ſo he called Mr. Firmin's ſon, who is mentioned in the ſecond chapter as dying when juſt ſetting out in life *.

The regard which the Archbiſhop ſhewed Mr. Firmin, purely on account of his many valuable qualities, expoſed him to the charge of being a Socinian at heart, an accuſation which was entirely groundleſs. But beſides his friendſhip with a chief of that party, he had given furious bigots no ſmall diſguſt, by candidly acknowledging that the Socinian writers diſplayed temper, judgment, and learning in the controverſy, between

* Life, page 15. 17. Birch's Life of Archbiſhop Tillotſon, page, 321.

them

them and the orthodox. This greatly offended all thoſe zealots, who will not allow an adverſary to have common ſenſe or common honeſty; but it had a very good effect on the minds of thoſe, whom he endeavoured to convince of an error. In the book, which Mr. Firmin cauſed to be drawn up in anſwer to his Sermons, he was ſtyled " the common " father of the nation, and is acknow- " ledged to have inſtructed the Socinians " themſelves, with the air and language " of a father, not of an adverſary or a " judge." And it was added " that they " were concerned for their own reputa- " tion to reverence his perſon and admo- " nitions." Of what unſpeakable ſervice would it be to the cauſe of charity and truth, if all controverſies were managed by perſons of ſuch temper and judgment.

The time, when Mr, Firmin was moſt active in his oppoſition to the doctrine of the Trinity, was the moſt favourable that could be to the views of the Unitarians, the defenders of the orthodox faith being greatly divided amongſt themſelves, ſome oppoſing, with much heat and virulence, the explanations which had been given by others. To give an account of the various ſolutions, which the advocates for the doctrine of the Trinity have offered by way of explaining this myſtery, would be only to ſet before the Reader, innumerable ſentences of unintelligible jargon, and which, as far as they can be underſtood, abſolutely contradict one another. Eſſences and exiſtencies, hypoſtaſes and perſonalities, priorities and coequalities, Unity in Plurality, and Trinity in Unity are but a few of the phraſes, which men have invented to expreſs their ideas on this ſubject. If it be a doctrine of revelation that there are "Three perſons in the Godhead, and "that theſe three are one God equal in "power and glory, the Son begotten of "the Father, and the Holy Ghoſt pro-"ceeding from the Father and the Son, "and yet none to be afore or after "another, none to be greater or leſs than "another:" If ſuch be the expreſs doctrine of revelation, yet all attempts to explain it only darken the matter; for language does not furniſh us with words to deſcribe, nor has the Divine Being given us ideas to comprehend it; and therefore all ſuch endeavours are un-

profitable

profitable and vain. However there were ſeveral divines, contemporaries with Mr. Firmin, who diſtinguiſhed themſelves by the various efforts which they made to render intelligible what all acknowledged to be a myſtery. Their different ſolutions only ſerved to puzzle the queſtion, and though all endeavoured to explain the thing, yet, as their definitions happened to be contradictory, they abuſed each other moſt heartily as heretics and infidels.

The chief of theſe renowned champions were the two celebrated doctors South and Sherlock. Both of them men of genius and learning, but each immoderately attached to his own peculiar notions, and bent upon defending them with all the fury, which theological zeal could inſpire. South's friends, who were the moſt numerous and powerful party, made complaint to the heads of the colleges at Oxford, the univerſity of which cenſured Sherlock's notions by a ſolemn decree in convocation, wherein they were declared to be "Falſe, impious "and heretical, and his book ordered to "be burned by the hands of the common "hangman." Sherlock treated the Oxford decree with the utmoſt contempt, retorting the charge of hereſy upon his antagoniſts; each party had their reſpective adherents, and in the courſe of the debate various ſolutions of the myſtery were propoſed by different writers, who maintained their reſpective and contradictory opinions with no ſmall degree of warmth and rancour. Theſe debates cauſed the Unitarian party to triumph not a little; for they thought it abſurd that they ſhould be condemned for not receiving a doctrine, which the moſt learned of its advocates could not agree in explaining, but on the contrary, treated each other as infidels, atheiſts and damnable heretics *. Whilſt ſo many reverend divines were abuſing each other, and making farther diviſions in the Chriſtian Church, Mr. Firmin, a private perſon and a tradeſman, endeavoured to the beſt of his abilities to promote peace and unity.

Thoſe who warmly contended for a Trinity of perſons in the Deity, yet differed greatly from one another about the meaning of the term perſon. Whilſt ſome

* Tindal's Continuation of Rapin, vol. III. page, 520, 21. and Burnet's Hiſtory of his own Times.

ſay that three divine perſons are three minds, ſpirits, ſubſtances and beings, eternal, infinite &c. others reject this as heresy, blaſphemy and tritheiſm. To reconcile the doctrine of the Trinity with the perfect unity of God, has perplexed the learned exceedingly; and various have been the phraſes and terms, which they have adopted. The unſcriptural expreſſions made uſe of in theſe debates, the Unitarians diſapproved; but they thought, that, notwithſtanding the learned had ſo greatly perplexed themſelves and their readers, the things intended by theſe terms were in fact agreeable to their ſentiments, or at leaſt that they might be allowed to uſe them in their own ſenſe. Such was the advantage which the Unitarians made of the diſputes amongſt their adverſaries, whoſe quarrels gave birth to the *Agreement between the Unitarians and the Catholic Church;* a book which was written chiefly at the inſtance of Mr. Firmin, in anſwer to ſeveral Trinitarian writers, who had charged his party with hereſy. After this treatiſe had been examined and corrected, it was publiſhed by Mr. Firmin, and that with more ſatisfaction than ever he had felt in ſending forth the many controverſial writings, which his ſincere love of truth had induced him to ſpread abroad in the world *. It is not to be wondered at, that a perſon of Mr. Firmin's diſpoſition, ſhould be ſo ready to embrace a reconciliation with the Church. He was ever a lover of peace, and always conformed as far as he could, according to that direction of the Apoſtle's, "Whereunto we have already attained, "let us walk by the ſame rule;" which he, with many learned interpreters underſtood thus, "conform to the doc-"trines, terms and uſages that are com-"monly received as far as you can; if in "ſome things you differ from the Church, "yet agree with her and walk by her "rule, to the utmoſt that in conſcience "you may." From this principle it was, that he never approved of a ſeparation from the Church, merely on account of ceremonies, habits, forms of goverment, or any of the bare circumſtantials of religion; and perſuaded many to conform, who objected nothing more to the eſtabliſhment than ſuch things as theſe †.

Chriſtians ſhould undoubtedly "ſtudy

* Life, page 20. † Life, page 21,

"the

" the things which make for peace" but if the beſt and moſt effectual way to reſtore peace, be to reſtore religion to its original ſimplicity and purity, thoſe ſeem to purſue the propereſt method, who refuſe to join, as ſtated worſhippers, with any Church whatſoever, which impoſes unſcriptural terms of conformity either on miniſters or people. Thoſe who peaceably diſſent from eſtabliſhments, and perſuade others to do ſo, may be as deſirous of unity and concord as thoſe who comply with them, and think they are purſuing a method moſt agreeable to the integrity required by the Goſpel. But though Mr. Firmin laid no ſtreſs on forms, and ceremonies, many, perhaps, will wonder, how he, being a Socinian, or, as it has been ſaid, an Arian *, could conform

* Dr. Birch aſſerts this in his Life of Archbiſhop Tillotſon, page 320. I ſuppoſe on the authority of Biſhop Burnet's Hiſtory of his own Times, vol. III. page 292. Whether Biſhop Burnet heard Mr. Firmin explain himſelf on this head, or received ſuch an account from ſome other hand he hath not told us. In all probability he was miſtaken. The books which Mr. Firmin diſtributed, favoured the Socinian ſcheme, which ſeems to have been adopted by all the Unitarians of that age. The Arians were hardly ever ſpoken of

conform to the Church in its worſhip. Much dexterity muſt certainly be neceſſary, to reconcile the Athanaſian creed with the belief of the perfect unity and abſolute unrivalled ſupremacy of the One God; and ſtill more to juſtify the offering up diſtinct prayers to three perſons, when he, who uſes theſe forms, means to addreſs one perſon only. Beſides, the conſtant repetition of theſe terms and phraſes muſt neceſſarily lead the greater part of mankind into ſentiments and ideas very oppoſite to thoſe which the Unitarian adopts concerning the Deity. How, then, can a ſincere lover of truth reconcile himſelf to the uſe of them? To all this it may be replied, with reſpect to Mr. Firmin, that his caſe was a very particular one. It does not appear that any Unitarian ſociety was kept up after the death of Mr. Biddle. The diſſenters of that age were not only Trinitarians, but likewiſe in general more attached to the Calviniſtical doctrines than the clergy, moſt of whom indeed rejected them.

of in England till Dr. Clarke and Mr. Whiſton were charged with reviving doctrines ſimilar to thoſe, which had been of old maintained by Arius and his followers.

The

The Quakers, besides renouncing the positive ordinances of christianity, were then very enthusiastical. Mr. Firmin was, therefore, under the disagreeable necessity of attending no public worship at all, or of joining where forms were used, and doctrines delivered, to which he had material objections. No wonder then that he endeavoured to reconcile himself to the use of some improper terms and expressions, rather than be deprived of all the pleasures of social devotion. Had he lived in these days, there is great reason to suppose, that he would have joined in communion with some of those private societies, where forms and expressions merely of human invention are exploded, and the one God and Father of all is worshipped through the one Mediator Jesus Christ, in whose name the assistance of the Blessed Spirit of grace and truth is humbly implored. Several clergymen, of most respectable and worthy characters, have within these few years thought it their duty to resign their preferments, rather than continue to join in forms which their consciences disapproved; and certainly this is acting a worthy and upright part*. Mr. Firmin pursued the course which he thought best, unbiassed by any regard to his private interest, or the apprehension of being thought singular. Those worldly considerations, which have great weight with many, had none with him. He was never ashamed of the Gospel of Christ, nor of those sentiments, which he had formed concerning it; but he ever avowed and did his best to support and countenance them.

But though, by taking advantage of the explanations, which some great divines had given of the Trinitarian doctrine, he thought he might venture to profess himself to be really of the same mind with the Catholic Church, and the Church of England, yet he resolved to continue his endeavours, "That no false notion of the Trinity should corrupt the sincere faith of "the Unity. He was persuaded that the article of the Unity is the first article of "Christianity, the article that distinguishes "Christians from Pagans: as the belief

* The names of Robertson, Lindsey, Jebb, and Evanson are well known, nor are these the only ones who have lately from motives of pure conscience left the established church.

" of the Meſſiah already come diſtin-
" guiſhes us from the Jews. He judged
" that though the unſcriptural terms Tri-
" nity, three divine perſons, and ſuch
" like, in the ſenſe they are intended by
" the Church, contain a doctrine which
" is true; yet taken in the ſenſe they
" bear in common familiar ſpeech, in
" which ſenſe the greater number of
" men (almoſt all the unlearned) muſt
" needs underſtand them; they imply
" a more groſs and abſurd polytheiſm,
" than any of the old heathens were
" guilty of. He that underſtands three
" Divine Perſons to be three (diſtinct,
" infinite, all perfect) ſpirits or beings,
" or minds, three creators, three ſeveral
" objects of worſhip, is more guilty of
" polytheiſm, than the Greeks or Romans
" ever were before their converſion to
" Chriſtianity. For though they and
" other nations were heathens, that is
" polytheiſts, aſſerters of more gods;
" yet they never believed more than one
" infinite, all perfect ſpirit, the father
" and king of the leſſer deities. Mr.
" Firmin knew well that the majority of
" vulgar chriſtians, and not a few lear-
" ed men, have tritheiſtic notions or
conception

" conceptions of the Trinity or three Di-
" vine Perſons each of which is God:
" namely, that they are three diſtinct,
" infinite, all perfect minds or ſpirits.
" Meeting this every day in converſation
" as well as in books, he was not leſs
" zealous for the doctrine of the Unity
" after the publication of the ſcheme of
" agreement than before; and therefore
" he propoſed, beſides the continuation of
" his former efforts, to hold aſſemblies
" for divine worſhip, diſtinct from the
" aſſemblies of any other denomination
" of chriſtians. But he did not intend
" theſe aſſemblies or congregations by
" way of ſchiſm or ſeparation from the
" Church; but only as *Fraternities in the*
" *Church*, who would undertake a more
" eſpecial care of that article, for the
" ſake of which it is certain both the
" Teſtaments were written. The great
" deſign and ſcope of both Teſtaments, and
" the reaſon that they were given by
" God, was to regain mankind to the
" belief and acknowledgment of but one
" God; to deſtroy polytheiſm of all ſorts.
" Mr. Firmin intended to recommend it
" to the Unitarian congregations, as the
" very reaſon of their diſtinct aſſembling,
" to

"to be particularly mindful of, and "zealous for, the article of the Unity, to "cause it to be so explained in their as-"semblies, catechisms and books (with-"out denying or so much as suppressing "the catholic doctrine of the Trinity) "that all men might easily and readily "know in what sense the Unity of God "is to be believed, and the mystery of a "Trinity of Divine Persons (each of "them God) is to be interpreted. Mr. "Firmin feared that without such as-"semblies, the continual use of terms, "which in their ordinary signification "are confessed by all to imply three "Gods, would paganize at some time "the whole Christian Church *.

This plan of Mr. Firmin's did not take place, for he died before it could well be put into execution. Many perhaps will be of opinion, that it was by no means a sufficient protest against the use of phrases, which were thought to have so direct a tendency to lead men into the belief of a doctrine, which subverted that important article the Unity of God. A total separation from all

* An account of Mr. Firmin's religion annexed to his Life, page 50. 51.

churches,

churches, where ſuch forms are uſed, ſeems to be the duty of every Unitarian; eſpecially if he live in a place where a Unitarian ſociety is or may be ſet on foot. Thoſe, who ſeparate from an eſtabliſhment, may ſtill be joined in affection and love to all its ſincere and pious members; for ſurely the warmeſt charity may, and oftentimes does ſubſiſt, between thoſe who worſhip in different places, and make uſe of different forms. A unity of ſounds in the bonds of ignorance, or a unity of practice in the bonds of hyprocriſy, is by no means deſireable. To promote a unity of ſpirit in the bonds of peace ſhould be the endeavour of all the ſincere inquirers after truth; and ſuch a unity will be moſt likely to ſubſiſt between thoſe, who, however they may differ from one another, are all impartial and upright in their reſearches.

Mr. Firmin, beſides his attachment to Mr. Biddle, evidenced in the early part of his life a generous regard for thoſe who ſuffered on account of their Unitarian opinions. It was in the year 1658, when he was a very young man, that the Unitarians were baniſhed from Poland. Thoſe who, about the time of the Reformation,

formation, firſt began to have doubts concerning the doctrine of the Trinity, were ſome learned and inquiſitive perſons in the ſtate of Venice, who held meetings where they converſed with freedom on religious ſubjects. Some of theſe by the vigilance of the Popiſh emiſſaries were ſeized and put to death, others fled to different countries, and Lælius Socinus, who was born of a moſt noble family, betook himſelf to Poland, and having inſtilled his ſentiments into the queen's confeſſor, who defended them in writing, they were adopted by ſeveral learned men. This was about the year 1558, and long before the celebrated Fauſtus Socinus * viſited that kingdom. As the Socinians increaſed in numbers and reputation, many privileges were granted to them about the year 1600, and ſeveral flouriſhing ſocieties were formed, protected, and countenanced by perſons of the higheſt rank. After having en-

* Such as are deſirous of knowing, what was the real character, and what were the real ſentiments of that noted man, may obtain full ſatisfaction from the very accurate and impartial account which Mr Toulmin hath given in his " Memoirs of the Life, Character, Sentiments and Writings of Fauſtus Socinus.

joyed

joyed honour and ſecurity for nearly threeſcore years, and diſtinguiſhed themſelves not a little by their many learned writings, a decree was made, and an edict iſſued out, by which all Unitarians, who would not embrace the Roman Catholic religion, were baniſhed out of Poland, two years being however allowed them to ſell their eſtates and effects *.

The Unitarians upon this left Poland and ſettled, ſome in Tranſylvania, where they had many friends, and others, in different places. Amongſt theſe were many poor perſons; and, therefore, ſuch of the nobility and gentry, as were of that perſuaſion, not being able in this perſecuted ſtate, to relieve the wants of their ſuffering brethren, applied for help to all the Unitarian churches in foreign parts. They knew, that in England a few families only had imbibed theſe ſentiments; yet they ſent a letter to entreat aſſiſtance; and Mr. Firmin procured contributions from ſome whom he knew to be well affected to them. And though no brief was granted, collections were made in a few of the churches, which

* Life of Mr. Firmin, page 23.

evidenced

evidenced a liberality of mind, in thoſe who encouraged them, very ſeldom to be met with in that age of bigotry. Mr. Firmin poſſeſſed this generoſity of ſoul in an eminent degree. It was without doubt natural for him to aſſiſt the perſecuted Unitarians; but about twenty years after, he had an opportunity of giving a remarkable proof of the unbounded extent of his charity.

In 1681, King Charles granted a brief to another ſort of Polonian ſufferers, who alſo were Proteſtants. They had permitted the Unitarians to be baniſhed, when it would have been effectually prevented, had but one of their deputies proteſted againſt it in the Diet (or general aſſembly of the ſtates) for perfect unanimity is indiſpenſably neceſſary amongſt the Poles to render any decree valid. The other Proteſtants thus willingly permitted, and even promoted that edict by which the Unitarians were ſentenced to baniſhment, and the natural conſequence of the loſs of ſo large and reſpectable a body was the weakening the reformed intereſt to ſuch a degree as enabled the Papiſts almoſt effectually to ruin it. The Calviniſts and Lutherans would not have loſt their

their liberty and their country, had they not voted themſelves out of both, when they conſented to the perſecution of the Unitarians; for the various ſects, when united, formed too ſtrong a party for the Papiſts to meddle with.

Mr. Firmin, however, exerted himſelf to give them ſupport under their troubles; and, as if he had forgotten the former injury which they had done his friends, or rather, influenced by that excellent precept of the Goſpel, not to render evil for evil, but to do good even to an enemy when in neceſſity, he kindly aſſiſted theſe perſecuted perſecutors. The ſum of five hundred and ſixty-eight pounds was paid in to him upon that account, beſides one hundred and ten pounds, being the contribution of nine diſſenting congregations *. It was much to the honour of the diſſenters, that they were thus diſpoſed to aſſiſt foreign ſufferers, when they themſelves had been ſo ſeverely harraſſed and perſecuted, and their liberty was ſo precarious. What enabled them to bear thoſe great expenſes which they ſuſtained by the ejec-

* Life, page 26.

tion

tion of their miniſters, and the heavy fines, which were from time to time laid both upon them and their hearers, was their extraordinary ſrugality and prudence. They loved the intereſt of religion, and dedicated to the ſervice of that what their poſterity ſeem moſt inclined to devote to expenſive faſhions and amuſements, a prevailing love of which will effectually ſuppreſs and eradicate every noble, generous, and manly ſentiment of the human heart.

Thus various and impartial, extenſive and liberal were Mr. Firmin's charities. It may well be ſuppoſed that only the moſt ſtriking particulars of an active life, almoſt entirely devoted to benevolent purpoſes, could be recorded. There is, however, one inſtance more of his goodneſs, which deſerves particular mention. When the money was called in, and there was a very great ſcarcity of current coin, that he might be able to continue his former charities, at a time when they were more needful than ever, he leſſened his own expenſes by laying down his coach *. This, conſidering his noble

* Life, page 77.

connections,

connections, and the vast business which required his attendance at different places, was no small sacrifice. If the admiration of the Reader be excited on a review of so many acts of true and disinterested benevolence, may that admiration tend to cherish in his breast the same godlike dispositions!

CHAP. VI.

Mr. Firmin's Sickneſs and Death. He is attended in his laſt Illneſs by Biſhop Fowler, of whom a ſhort Account is given. The Reſpect paid to Mr. Firmin's Memory by Lady Clayton. Reflections on his Character, with ſome Extracts from a Sermon preached on Occaſion of his Deceaſe.

THE ſhortneſs of human life has been a frequent ſubject of complaint; and thoſe whoſe vices have inclined them to infidelity, and diſpoſed them to ſeek for arguments, which might ſerve to excuſe their contempt of religion, have alledged this as a reaſon againſt the doctrine of Providence. But it is a high degree of folly and preſumption to argue in this manner: we are very incompetent judges of what in this caſe is right and fit. We may be aſſured that the period allotted to us by the great Giver of life is fully ſufficient for our performing all that he expects we ſhould do. A ſhort

 exiſtence

existence in this state is too long for those who are bent on wicked courses; mankind have no reason to wish for their stay in it. A life of labour and toil, of pain and sorrow, which falls to the lot of many, cannot be very desirable. And with respect to the benevolent and virtuous, who are blessings to their friends and to society, they are convinced that God expects them to do no more good in the world, when he sees fit to take them out of it; and they have no cause to repine at being soon called to receive the reward of their labours. Mankind, when they lament the loss of such, ought not to reflect upon the Divine Wisdom, but learn to be wise themselves; for there would not be so much cause to lament the removal of the good, if more would learn to imitate their worthy actions.

Dear and valuable as Mr. Firmin's life was, yet it could not reasonably be expected, that it should extend much beyond the common period allotted to mortality; and, if those who loved him, fondly indulged such a hope, they were greatly disappointed, for he did not reach seventy. His constitution was naturally strong and firm; but he had greatly weakened it by a constant a conſtant and unremitting attention to his many and various charitable employments. He ſeemed to have adopted the maxims of the excellent Biſhop Cumberland, who lived to be eighty-ſeven, and could not, even in his very laſt month, be diſſuaded from undertaking fatigues though ſuperior to his ſtrength, his anſwer and reſolution was, "I will do my duty as "long as I can:" and when his friends repreſented to him, that ſo much ſtudy and labour would injure his health, his uſual reply was, "A man had better "wear out, than ruſt out."

"Mr. Firmin was ſometimes liable to "jaundices, often afflicted with cholics, "and was ſcarcely ever without a cough, "for his lungs had been long ptyſical. "He would often return home ſo tired "and depreſſed in his ſpirits, that his pulſe "were ſcarcely to be felt, or very languid; "and he would then take a little reſt in "his chair, but ſoon ſtart up out of it "and appear very lively in company, eſ-"pecially where any good was to be "done. The more immediate cauſe of "his death was a fever which ſeized his "ſpirits, beginning with a chillneſs and "ſhivering, and then a heat enſued. He "was at the ſame time afflicted both in "his lungs, with a great ſhortneſs of "breath, not having ſtrength to expecto-"rate, and alſo with ſuch terrible pains "in his bowels that for many hours "nothing could be made to paſs through "him. He had alſo for many years been "troubled with a large rupture, all "which made his ſickneſs very ſhort. He "had wiſhed in his lifetime that he "might not lie above two days on a "dying bed; God granted to him his "deſire, he lay not ſo long by eight hours, "and December 20th, about two of the "o'clock in the morning, anno dom. 1697, "he died."

During his laſt illneſs, he was viſited by his moſt dear friend Biſhop Fowler; but on account of the extreme violence of his pains, he could hold but little converſe with him. What did paſs between them his Lordſhip made known under his own hand, and was as follows. "Mr. "Firmin told me he was now going: "and I truſt," ſaid he, "God will not "condemn me to worſe company than I "have loved and uſed in the preſent life." I replied, "That he had been an extra-"ordinary example of charity, the poor "had

"had a wonderful blessing in you: I "doubt not these works will follow you, "if you have no expectation from the "merit of them, but rely on the infinite "goodness of God, and the merits of our "Saviour." Here he answered "I do so: "and I say in the words of my Saviour, "*When I have done all, I am but an unpro-* "*fitable servant.* He was in such an agony "of body for want of breath, that I did "not think fit to speak more to him, but "only to give him assurance of my earn- "est prayers for him, while he remained "in this world. Then I took a solemn "and affectionate farewel of him, and he "of me *."

"It

* Bishop Fowler was a man well deserving particular notice in a life of Mr. Firmin *. He was born in the year 1632, at Westerleigh in Gloucestershire, and received his grammar learning at the college school in Gloucester. In 1650, he became clerk of Corpus Christi College in Oxford, of which he was admitted as a chaplain three years after, being very ready and fluent in extemporary prayer. On Bartholomew day, 1662, he was ejected from the rectory of Northall in Bedfordshire, to which he had been presented by the Countess of Kent †. However, not being willing to lie in silence and obscurity, he endeavoured to

* Life, page 81—3.

† Nonconformist's Memorial, vol. I. page 225.

 conquer

" It is usual to conclude lives with a
" character of the persons, both as to
" their bodies and the qualities of their
" minds: therefore I must further add.
" Mr. Firmin was of a low stature, well
" proportioned; his complexion fair and
" bright;

conquer his scruples; and after a while, having reconciled himself to the imposed terms, he conformed and became a great ornament to the church. His father, who was eminent both for ministerial abilities and labours, and his brother, who had a valuable living of three hundred pounds per ann. and shortened his days by a close application to study, were both ejected at the same time *, and could never bring their consciences to submit to the act of uniformity. But it does not appear that ever they censured him, who did comply: nor had they cause, men of equal learning, piety, and integrity may see the same thing in different lights. Mr. Fowler having distinguished himself by some excellent moral writings, Archbishop Sheldon was desirous of introducing him to the metropolis of the kingdom; and, therefore, in August 1673, gave him the rectory of All-hallows, Bread-Street. In 1675, he was made prebendary of Gloucester; and in March 1681, vicar of St. Giles, Cripplegate.

In this respectable situation he made himself very obnoxious to the court and its adherents, by his strenuous opposition to Popery. Some of his parishioners also, in order to recommend themselves to the higher powers, commenced an ill-natured prosecution against

* Nonconformist's Memorial, vol. I. page 549. and vol. II. page 218.

him;

" bright; his eye and countenance lively, " his aſpect manly and promiſing ſome- " what extraordinary, ſo that a ſtranger " might readily take him for a man of " good ſenſe, worth, and dignity. Walk- " ing or ſitting he appeared more comely " than

him; alledging that he was guilty of Whiggiſm, and that he admitted to the communion excommunicated perſons, before they were abſolved; and the matter being tried at Doctor's Commons, he was ſuſpended. This affront, however, did not intimidate him; for he went on in the reſolute performance of his duty, and was the ſecond who ſigned the reſolution, into which many of the London clergy entered, not to read King James's declaration for liberty of conſcience. On account of this and his excellent writings, which did honour to the church and nation; he was preferred by King William, in 1691, to the See of Glouceſter, in which he continued till his death, in Auguſt 1714, having reached his 82d year *.

Biſhop Fowler had the cauſe of rational piety and practical religion much at heart; and he thought the main deſign of Chriſtianity was to promote real holineſs. He was no zealot for mere outward forms; and expoſed himſelf to the rage of furious bigots, by writing in defence of thoſe divines, who were then ſtyled Latitudinarians. Thoſe who were thus denominated, were accuſed of Socinianiſm, Atheiſm, &c. for no other reaſon than their explaining ſome doctrines in a manner leſs myſterious than had been uſual amongſt divines, and alſo becauſe they were ready to ſacrifice

* Biographical Dictionary, Article Fowler.

" than ſtanding ſtill; for his mien and " action gave a gracefulneſs to his perſon. " The endowments, inclinations, and " qualities of his mind, the reader may " form a judgment of from the account " which hath been given of his life. It " appears that he was quick of appre- " henſion and diſpatch, and yet almoſt in- " defatigably induſtrious, properties that " very rarely meet in the ſame man. He " was beſides inquiſitive and very inge- " nious, he had a thirſt after knowledge, " and the quickneſs of his underſtanding " enabled him to acquire it in a large de- " gree, with but little labour. He could " not diſſemble; on the contrary, his " love or anger, his liking or diſlike, " might be eaſily perceived. In both theſe " reſpects he was rather too open, but open- " neſs is the effect of ſincerity and the ar- " gument of an honeſt mind. He never " proudly affected the notice of others,

a few ceremonies and rites, confeſſedly indifferent in their nature, rather than exclude from the church many excellent perſons, who ſcrupled to ſubmit to the impoſition of them. Biſhop Fowler was a learned advocate for the doctrine of the Trinity. The mutual eſteem between him and Mr. Firmin aroſe from the warm love which they both had for real piety and goodneſs wherever found.

" whether

" whether above or below him, which " ſeems a good proof that his charities " did not proceed from any affectation of " honour or glory amongſt men, but from " the love of God, and his afflicted brother. " He was naturally facetious, but he " valued judgment rather than wit. He " was neither preſuming or over bold, " nor yet timorous; a little prone to an- " ger, but never exceſſive in it either as " to meaſure or time. Being well aſſured " in himſelf of his own intregrity, he " heard without uneaſineſs the calumnies " which ſome malicious perſons had pro- " pagated concerning him, only he was " ſorry that men ſhould be ſo wicked and " raſh as to invent or report falſehoods and " lies merely to gratify a malignant or " envious diſpoſition *."

He had often ſignified, that it was his deſire to be buried in Chriſt Church Hoſpital, the intereſts of which charitable inſtitution he appeared to have much at heart when living. In compliance with this his deſire, he was interred in the cloyſters of that Hoſpital, and his relatives

* Life, p. 83,—4. The above quotation is not ſtrictly literal, a few alterations were made with a view to convey the ſame ſenſe the more clearly.

erected a marble to his memory, with the following inscription.

UNDER that stone, near this place, lyeth the body of Thomas Firmin, late Citizen of London, a Governour of this and St. Thomas's Hospital; who by the Grace of God, was created in Christ Jesus unto good works, wherein he was indefatigably industrious, and successfully provoked many others thereto, becoming also their Almoner, visiting and relieving the Poor at their Houses, and in prisons, whence also he redeemed many. He set many hundreds of them at work, to the expending of great stocks: he rebuilt, repaired, and added conveniences to Hospitals, weekly overseeing the Orphans. The Refugees from France, and from Ireland, have partaken largely, the effects of his Charity, Pains, and earnest Solicitations for them. He was wonderfully Zealous in every good Work, beyond the Example of any in our age. Thus shewed he his Faith by his Works, and cannot reasonably be reproached for that which brought forth such plenty of Good Fruits.

He died Dec. 20, 1697, *and in the* 66*th year of his Age* *.

* Life, p. 89, 90.

Lady

Lady Clayton had ſo great a reſpect for his memory, that, with the concurrence of Sir Robert, ſhe erected a handſome monument in their garden at Marden in Surry, in a walk called *Mr. Firmin's Walk*, he being the perſon who had planned it. This monument is a marble pillar, about eight feet high, with an urn and flowers growing out of the top of it, with this moto, *Floreſcit funere virtus.* there is alſo a marble table fixed to one ſide of the pillar, with the following inſcription.

To perpetuate (as far as Marble and Love can do it) the Memory of Thomas Firmin Citizen of London.

None ever paſſed the ſeveral periods of Human Life more irreproachably, or perform'd the common Duties of Society with greater ſincerity and approbation. Though it appears, by his public ſpirit, that he thought himſelf born rather for the Benefit of others, than his own private Advantage; yet the ſatisfaction of doing Good, and the univerſal eſteem of honeſt men, made him the happieſt perſon in the world. But his Charity (which was not confined to any Nation, Sect, or Party) is most worthy thy Imitation, at least in some Degree, O Reader! He was as liberal of his own, as faithful in distributing the pious Donations of others whom he successfully persuaded to relieve the distressed, particularly the laborious poor; for of vagrant, idle, and insolent Beggars, he was no advocate nor encourager. His agreeable Temper rendered him an extraordinary lover of Gardens, he contrived this Walk, which bears his Name, and where his improving Conversation and Example are still remembered. But since Heaven has better disposed of him, this Pillar is erected to Charity and Friendship by Sir Robert Clayton, and Martha his Lady, who first builded and planted in Marden.

Born at Ipswich, in Suffolk.
Buried in Christ Church Hospital London.

Gardening was the amusement in which Mr. Firmin chiefly delighted. The author of his life says " He cultivated a piece of ground at Hoxton, not " a mile from London, where he raised " flowers, and in time attained no small " skill in the art of gardening, in the " culture of flowers, herbs, greens, and " fruit

" fruit trees of all ſorts. I have often
" borne him company to his garden; but
" either going, or coming back, he uſed
" often to viſit the poor and ſick: this
" was one of Mr. Biddle's leſſons, that
" it is a duty not only to relieve, but
" to viſit the ſick and poor; becauſe
" they are hereby encouraged and com-
" forted, and we come to know more of
" what nature and degree their ſtraits
" are, and that ſome are more worthy
" of aſſiſtance than others; and their con-
" dition being known, ſometimes we are
" able to aſſiſt them by our counſel, or
" our intereſt, much more effectually
" than by the charity we do or can be-
" ſtow upon them *.

" Such were the general endeavours and
" performances of Mr. Firmin's life.
" The particulars under each general
" head were ſo numerous, that to relate
" them all would perhaps tire both the
" Reader and the Writer. We have taken
" a view, though but an imperfect one, of
" a perſon of middle extraction and ſlen-
" der beginnings, who raiſed himſelf to
" the honour of a very great number of

* Life, p. 10.

" illuſtrious friendſhips, and to an afflu-
" ence of worldly wealth; to which
" when he had attained by induſtry,
" integrity, and worth, like our Saviour,
" he went about doing good. In reſpect
" of his endeavours in all kinds of cha-
" rity, he may deſervedly be called *the*
" *Father of the Poor*, and with regard to
" the Iriſh and French refugees, *the Almo-*
" *ner of England.* The Divine hand had
" qualified him to do much good, him-
" ſelf ſought out the objects and occa-
" ſions for it, and delighted in the work.
" And he did it with ſo much diligence
" and application that he might even
" have ſaid with our Saviour, *my meat is*
" *to do the will of him that ſent me; and*
" *to finiſh his Work.*

" The Jeſuit, who aſſiſted the late fa-
" mous Marſhal Luxemburgh in his laſt
" hours, thought he might well put this
" queſtion to him: Well, Sir, tell me,
" had you not rather now to have given
" one alms to a poor man, in his diſtreſs
" for God's ſake, than to have won ſo
" many victories in the field of battle?
" the Marſhal confeſſed he ſhould now
" chooſe the former, ſeeing nothing will
" avail any man, in the eternal world,
" but

" but only the actions of charity, or
" of juſtice and piety. The confeſſor
" doth not ſeem to have been imperti-
" nent in the queſtion; for in our ſerious
" laſt hours we ſhall all be ſenſible,
" and be likewiſe ready to confeſs, that
" we were wiſe only in that part of our
" life which was laid out in the duties
" either of humanity towards men, or
" piety towards God. The Craſſi and
" Crœſi, the Hannibals and Luxemburghs,
" the moſt conſpicuous for wealth or mi-
" litary glory, how gladly would they in
" their expiring moments, exchange all the
" fruits of their ambition, for ſome part
" of our Firmin's toil and labour for the
" poor, and the deſerving. Is it for
" want of *faith* or of *conſideration*, that
" we are ſo better pleaſed with read-
" ing the acts of the Alexanders, the
" Charlemains, and other falſe heroes,
" than thoſe of perſons who have been
" exemplary for juſtice, beneficence or
" devotion, and are now triumphant in
" heaven on the account of thoſe ſervices
" to God and to men? but ſo it is, either
" becauſe we are not *Chriſtians* or be-
" cauſe we are, *fools;* we are, commonly
" ſpeaking,

" ſpeaking, better pleaſed with the ſons of " earth than of heaven *."

It is to be hoped, that the Readers of Mr. Firmin's life, whoever they may be, will learn to value and to imitate ſo exalted a character, and be confirmed and ſtrengthened in the beſt and worthieſt diſpoſitions, eſpecially in humanity, and charity. Mr. Firmin affords the beſt example on record to young tradeſmen. Such may learn what vaſt ſervice one of but ſmall fortune was capable of doing, by ſtriving to merit the acquaintance of ſuch perſons of rank and eminence as were enabled and diſpoſed to do good. Many, who have ſufficient wealth to render them extenſively and eminently uſeful to their fellow creatures, would be really ſo, did ſome active perſons of known ability and integrity ſtir them up to it by their examples and ſolicitations: Mr. Firmin was a great maſter of the art of perſuaſion. He poſſeſſed a conſiderable degree of prudence as well as wit and addreſs, and knew how to chooſe the *mollia tempora fandi*, the fitteſt ſeaſons for ſpeaking, and when he ſpoke, he ap-

* Life, p. 77,—9, the quotation is not quite literal.

plied

plied himſelf to thoſe paſſions of the perſon whom he ſolicited which could moſt effectually be wrought upon. He once went to aſk a citizen of the higheſt rank, for his charity towards rebuilding St. Thomas's hoſpital, and petitioned him for no leſs than one hundred pounds. This citizen having been ſome way or other diſobliged by the governors of the hoſpital, refuſed to ſubſcribe any thing. But Mr. Firmin ſeeing him one day in company with ſome friends, whom he reſpected, and by whom he was willing to be reſpected, and alſo finding that he was in a very good humour, he again renewed his requeſt, and by this well timed application obtained the whole ſum which he had deſired *. To his perſonal ſolicitations he was ſometimes forced to add letters; and frequently ſucceeded beſt by the arguments there made uſe of. It appears, by one of his books, dated 1679, that he had received the ſum of five hundred and twenty pounds from ſeventy-two perſons, and in the year 1681, the ſum of five hundred and thirty-two pounds from forty-three

* Life, p. 47.

persons. All these were to be treated with privately, as opportunity offered; which required much time, caution, industry and discretion, which laid out on his own business must have been of vast private advantage. Mr. Firmin might much more easily have been one of the great men of the world, than almoner general for the poor and the hospitals *. Thus it was, that, though he was a great master of the art of persuasion, his actions always spoke with more eloquence and force than his words: and as he never thought any thing, which he could say or do, was too much, when charity was the subject, he met with uncommon success in his applications. But lessons of benevolence and humanity are not the only ones which we may learn from a review of Mr. Firmin's character. What was it which made him so active, so useful, and so exemplary? it was a principle of religion. The feelings, natural to the human heart, may excite a man to relieve a distressed object, who appears in view; but to be incessantly seeking out for such, and labouring for

* Life p. 48.

their good, to ſacrifice not only riches, but alſo many of the comforts of life, to waſte the ſtrength and health in the ſervice of ſtrangers and foreigners, theſe are actions which clearly prove that the mind is actuated by religious motives. And. what religion is ſo well adapted to render a man unwearied in well doing as the religion of Jeſus? and what more excellent definition can be given of religion than that which we have in one of the ſacred writers? *Pure religion and undefiled before God and the Father is this, to viſit the Fatherleſs and Widows in their affliction, and to keep himſelf unſpotted from the world* *. The excellent nature and happy tendency of this religion Mr. Firmin underſtood and felt; and he was unwearied in his endeavours to promote the knowledge of it in its purity and the practice of it in its fulleſt extent. And what but a ſecret love to vice, of ſome one vice at leaſt, or a moſt unaccountable turn of mind can render any perſon, who loves his fellow creatures, an enemy to the Goſpel of Jeſus Chriſt? this Goſpel contains the moſt excellent rules;

* James, i. 27.

it fets before us the moft perfect example; and the rewards which are promifed to a patient continuance in well-doing, afford the moft powerful motives which can be offered, to raife in the human heart the warmeft regard to every thing great and noble. The characters, which have been formed upon the Gofpel model, will appear upon examination to have been the moft uniformly good and ufeful which have ever been exhibited to the world. And the review of fuch a character as Mr. Firmin's cannot fail of exciting in every virtuous mind, an increafing love and reverence for that religion, which laid the foundation of fo many worthy and generous deeds.

If any, who read his life, fhould be inclined to think unfavourably of Mr. Firmin on account of his religious fentiments, (which on fome controverted points, were very different from thofe contained in the creeds and confeffions generally ftyled orthodox) let them only lay afide their prejudices in favour of a particular fyftem, and they will fee and acknowledge his worth. Some, who ftyle themfelves minifters of the Gofpel of peace,

peace, will yet take upon them in moſt of their public diſcourſes, rashly to condemn thoſe, who cannot aſſent to their explanations on doubtful and myſterious points. By this means many ſerious and well diſpoſed perſons are led to think unfavourably, and to ſpeak harſhly of thoſe, who differ from them. It is to be lamented that the men, who are zealous for controverted doctrines, about which there have been almoſt endleſs diſputes, ſhould at the ſame time be forgetful of this plain precept of their Redeemer, *Judge not that ye be not judged* *. Such may very properly be aſked in the language of the Apoſtle Paul, *Who art thou that judgeſt another man's ſervant? to his own maſter he ſtandeth or falleth* †. If men bring forth the fruits of righteouſneſs in their conduct and behaviour, how dare we to call in queſtion the ſincerity of their faith? This is ſetting up ourſelves for judges of the heart, which is the ſole prerogative of God. We may be aſſured, that He, being infinitely wiſe and good, though He may not ſee fit to guard his creatures againſt every miſtake, yet will

* Mat. vii. 1. † Rom. xiv. 4.

not ſuffer thoſe, who appear ſincerely deſirous of knowing and doing his will to fall into any fatal error *. A little acquaintance with the hiſtory of religion, and with the worthy characters of perſons differing from each other in ſpeculative

* Very pertinent to this matter are the ſentiments contained in a ſermon occaſioned by the death of Mr. Firmin, and affixed to his Life. It appears from the title page to have been preached in the country; but where, or by whom, it is not ſaid. In all probability it was delivered to ſome little private ſociety of Unitarians, who might perhaps have ventured to hold one ſecret meeting, that they might ſtir up each other to imitate the exupllencies of their departed friend, who had done their cauſe ſo much honour, and who was worthy of general imitation. Happy no doubt would they have thought themſelves, if the ſpirit of the times had permitted their more publicly aſſembling. The text was very ſuitable to the occaſion; Luke, x. 36, 37. *Which of theſe three, thinkeſt thou, was neighbour to him that fell among the thieves? He anſwered, he that ſhewed mercy on him. Then ſaid Jeſus, go and do thou likewiſe.* On theſe words the preacher made a number of uſeful and practical obſervations, of which the following may not be improperly quoted. " The cauſe of ſo great an averſion and diſpleaſure " between the Samaritans and Jews, was difference " of religion. The Samaritans owned only the firſt " five books of Holy Scripture, namely the books " written by Moſes. As to the prophets, the books " of Solomon, the Pſalms of David, Job, the books " of Kings and Chronicles, Nehemiah, Ezra, Ruth, " Eſther: theſe they received not as *divine books.*

" There

lative points, will tend to banish all narrow prejudices from the pious and good of every denomination, and they will learn to love one another with a pure heart fervently. Heaven is large enough to contain all the sincere friends of truth and

" There is no doubt that, in these matters, the Sama-
" ritans were to blame, and were in the wrong; the
" Jews had the advantage in all points that were con-
" troverted between them and the Samaritans. Nay
" farther, the Samaritans mistook even about the ob-
" ject of worship, God. Their notions or apprehen-
" sions of God, seem to have been confused and un-
" certain. They are the words of our Saviour, John
" iv. 22. *Ye* (ye Samaritans) *know not what ye wor-*
" *ship*; *we* (we Jews) *know what we worship*. The
" error then of the Samaritans consisted, not only in
" refusing diverse books, belonging to the Old Testa-
" ment, but their conceptions or opinions concerning
" God were not clear or true. Ye know not, says our
" Saviour, what ye worship; that is, ye know not
" God: some knowledge ye have of him, but ye know
" him not rightly: it is an obscure, confused, and
" for the most part of it, a mistaken knowledge that
" ye have of him.

" Of this nation, and of this religion, was the per-
" son whom our text so much commends. This is he
" of whom our Saviour says here, he was the true
" neighbour; the person whom the law of God in-
" tends when it says, *Thou shalt love thy neighbour as*
" *thyself*. He was not a Jew, that is, he was not of
" the true church of God: he owned but a small
" part of Holy Scriptures, disowning the far greater
" part of the Divine Word. His knowledge of the
" object

and virtue; and however such may differ in lesser matters, their views are all directed to the same end, and they are all going to the same place. Mr. Firmin thus humble, though at the same time with a rational confidence, expressed his

" object of worship, of God, was so imperfect, uncer-
" tain and confused, that our Saviour himself pro-
" nounces, the men of that religion knew not God.
" But with all these infelicities he was a doer of good,
" a lover of men, adorned with beneficent, charitable
" principles. Not carried away by the common
" and general example, whether of the Samaritans
" or Jews, to hate others merely for their religion;
" open handed and well affected to men as men. Such
" a one, says our Saviour in this text, is to be ac-
" counted a neighbour, he belongs to that charge
" and law of God, *thou shalt love thy neighbour as*
" *thyself*. A Levite, or Priest, though he is a mini-
" ster of God Most High, may less deserve the be-
" nefit of that law; he may not have so good a claim
" to it, as a man of a *far* country, and *another* reli-
" gion; the good man, the doer of good, is that
" person who only can challenge it as his right, to be
" loved as ourselves. Give me leave to make these
" few short remarks hereupon.

1st. " Our most blessed Saviour prefers here the
" Samaritan before the Levite, and the Priest; the
" doer of good before the man of right faith or true
" opinions: the reason is a man's faith, his right sect
" or way of religion, why, it is a desireable thing, a
" valuable felicity; but it does good to nobody but to
" the person himself. If I hold the true religion in
" all respects, so as not to mistake so much as in one
" point:

his hopes of happiness in his expiring moments; "I trust (said he) that God "will not condemn me to worse company than I have loved and used in the "present life." His delight had been in the company and converse of the excellent

"point: what is the world, what is my neighbour "the better for my great and exact knowledge and "skill? But if, like the Samaritan in this text, I am "a lover of men, a doer of good, open handed; or "if I cannot do so, yet open hearted; a great many "others one time or other shall be the better for this. "We cannot reasonably wonder that God esteems a "virtue which is useful to many, before a right faith, or "true knowledge, which are not a common and general good, as the doing of good is.

"2d. Again I take notice, it is not indeed in every "one's powers to do, as this Samaritan, to relieve the "poor or distressed in their wants, or to encourage the "worthy and deserving in their excellent endeavours. "But though few of us have the Samaritan's purse, all "may, and should, have his spirit. We can all of us "countenance, and be of party with the well deserving; "and the poor we can all of us help by our counsel, "favour, good looks and good words. There is no "commandment of God but all persons may earn "the recompence that belongs to it; for all of us can "perform it either in act, or by approving, applauding and favouring it. I make the deed of this "Samaritan, nay, all the best deeds of all other public "spirited, well-disposed men to be mine, if wanting "their wealth or their opportunities, I esteem the "persons for their actions, the men for what they do, lent of the earth, and ſuch he hoped would be his companions through eternity.

How rational, and at the ſame time how noble and exalted, are the views and proſpects of a ſincere chriſtian! If it be

" or have done. The firſt beginnings of excellent " virtue of whatſoever kind, are uſually in our appro- " bation of theſe kind of actions.

" 3d. Not the Levite, not the Prieſt, ſays our " Saviour have, but the Samaritan, the doer of good, " is that neighbour whom by God's law thou art to " love as thyſelf. It is true the Samaritan is of " another religion, he is ſo overſeen as not to own " ſome books that are genuine parts of Holy " Scripture: nay he has great miſtakes about the very " object of worſhip, about the very perſon of God; " his conceptions of God are ſo confuſed and uncer- " tain, that he worſhips he knows not well what. " For all that I ſay to thee, ſeeing he is an uſeful man, " full of good works, thou art to love him as thyſelf, " his ſtrange country or his miſtaken religion not- " withſtanding. But here what ſay ſome men? what, " embrace a Samaritan, a heretic, a man of falſe " religion? we have learned better things, and that " from Holy Scripture, from the Word of God itſelf. " *A man that is an heretic after the firſt and ſecond* " *admonition reject*, *Tit.* iii. 10. that is, caſt him off, " have nothing to do with him, avoid him as a peſt. " It is too common among the contending parties of " chriſtians, to take ſcripture words and names, and " having put them on the wrong perſon or ſubject, " to conclude preſently, we have confuted and " ſhamed be indeed possible for two or three in an age, after having imbibed the celebrated Mr. Hume's principles, to quit the world like their master. If this might happen to be the case in a few, a very few instances, where, owing to moderate passions,

" shamed them. A heretic, says the Apostle, reject him, " cast him off. Right! But then let us mean what " heretic he means. He means factious persons, " whether they be of a right or of a wrong opinion " in religion. To say it in few words, heresy is bigotry, " or faction; and heretic is a bigot, a factious or tur- " bulent person, whether such person happens to be " right or wrong in his opinions. *Hæreses sunt* " *placita vehementias defensa*, says a most learned " critic: heresy is any opinion, whether in philosophy, " religion, or politics, for which men contend too " earnestly and fiercely. It is not then the truth or " falsehood of any opinion that makes it to be heresy, " and the person that holds it a heretic, it is the stir, " clamour, and bustle made about it by any, that " makes the opinion heresy, and the man a heretic: " concerning such men the Apostle directs well, " *reject them* after having admonished them once " and again of their dangerous warmth, avoid them, " have no more to do with them. But as for others " who are mistaken, that is, we think they are mistaken " in their doctrines, the charge concerning them is " not to reject them or avoid them. On the contrary, we " are cautioned not to judge them, not to condemn " them; and for this reason, because they erring con- " scientiously, God receives them, God accepts them, " God will uphold them. Rom. xiv. 4. In short, ſions, or few temptations, no atrocious acts have been committed to alarm the conſcience in a dying hour; ſuppoſing that ſuch an one, not having formed the dear and tender connections of a huſband and a father, might be able to quit life with a calm indifference; yet as we are all liable to be drawn aſide ſo as to commit vices injurious to our own peace and the good order of ſociety, muſt not the reſtraints of religion be very uſeful? if an effectionate wife, a venerable parent, or a train of little helpleſs innocents, over whom his heart yearns with the fondeſt affection, attend the bed of an expiring mortal; if ſuch weep over his languiſhing body, and with all the eloquence of

" they ſay a heretic is to be rejected. I anſwer yes, " every bigot, every turbulent perſon, every fire-" brand, of whatſoever ſect or perſuaſion. But for " heretics that are commonly ſo miſcalled, that is, " perſons erring in doctrine, it will but ill become us " to reject them when the Holy Scriptures aſſure us in " expreſs terms that God accepts them." Theſe obſervations were much more juſt and liberal, than they were common at the time of their being delivered; and though it is to be hoped that a much better ſpirit prevails now, yet leſſons of charity and moderation can hardly be too often inculcated. This may excuſe the length of the quotation, which is but an abridgement of the preacher's arguments.

grief,

grief, bemoan his approaching end, can he *calmly* consign them over to fate and chance, and no one knows what, or cheerfully welcome the approach of death, which will carry him he knows not whither?

Oh Scepticism! poor and feeble must be thy aid in such circumstances, unless thy disciple have a heart of stone! But Christianity affords the most noble consolations at all seasons. The believer is persuaded, that, though he leaves a helpless offspring, the Father of the universe will be their friend; and as to himself, he hath a good hope, that pleasures are in store for him much more sublime and noble than this world can afford. In heaven the good are assured not only of an eternal exemption from pain and sorrow, but likewise of the fruition of every thing, which can administer joy to their souls. As to the pleasures of society and friendship they will undoubtedly enjoy them in a most exalted degree. All the children of God will then make but one family; the pious and good (and amongst these may be reckoned the most accomplished and learned of every age and of every

every country) will meet together in thoſe bleſt abodes.

Renowned warriors, who have fought, not as ambition, but as the duty they owed to their country and to mankind prompted them, will with ſatisfaction review, and with pleaſure recount their exploits; philoſophers, who ſtudied the works of creation, with a deſire of manifeſting the divine wiſdom, will be able to unfold all the ſecrets of nature; and perhaps be conveyed (if they wiſh it) as quick as thought from ſtar to ſtar, and from world to world.

Poets, who have devoted their talents to ſerve the intereſts of virtue, will there tune the praiſes of the Moſt High on immortal lyres; and the miniſters and friends of religion, who have ſincerely endeavoured to promote juſtice, purity, benevolence, and love, will there, with one heart and with one ſoul, join in thoſe aſcriptions of praiſe which are ſo juſtly due; *To the King Eternal, Immortal, Inviſible, the only Wiſe God;* and *to Jeſus the Prince of the Kings of the Earth, who loved us and waſhed us from our ſins in his own blood.*

Such

Such are the reflections, which naturally ariſe to the mind on contemplating the ſeveral parts of his conduct, whoſe life is the ſubject of this book. Happy will he be, who has attempted to ſet before mankind ſo ſhining a pattern of diſintereſted benevolence, and to revive the memory of one, in whom were united, to ſuch a remarkable degree, the moſt amiable and uſeful qualities, which can adorn humanity, if but one perſon be wrought upon to aſpire after an imitation of thoſe various excellencies, which joined in forming the character of

MR. THOMAS FIRMIN.

THE END.

Lately Publiſhed.

1. A Serious and earneſt Addreſs to Proteſtant Diſſenters of all Denominations, repreſenting the many and important Principles on which their Diſſent from the Eſtabliſhment is founded. The third Edition. Price 4d. or 3s. 6d. per dozen.

2. A Brief and impartial Hiſtory of the Puritans, repreſenting their Principles and Sufferings. With occaſional obſervations. Price 4d. or 3s. 6d. per dozen.

3. A Blow at the Root of all Prieſtly Claims. Price 1s. 6d.

4. A Letter to the Right Reverend the Lord Biſhop of Carliſle, containing a few Remarks on ſome Paſſages of his Lordſhip's Pamphlet entitled, "Conſiderations on the "Propriety of Requiring a Subſcription "to Articles of Faith." Price 1s.

N. B. The deſign of this Letter is to ſhew, that ſuch clergymen as with his Lordſhip, regard Subſcription to Human Articles of Faith, as an unwarrantable encroachment on Chriſtian Liberty, ought not on any account whatſoever to make ſuch Subſcription, and the total inſufficiency of the pleas which his Lordſhip makes in behalf of ſuch conduct is endeavoured to be proved.

The above Pamphlets are all written by JOSEPH CORNISH, and Printed for, J. JOHNSON, No, 72, St. Paul's Church-yard.

www.ingramcontent.com/pod-product-compliance
Lightning Source LLC
Chambersburg PA
CBHW030554040726
47497CB00008B/2713

* 9 7 8 3 3 3 7 3 3 3 2 3 2 *